JOHNNY HANGTIME

DAN GUTMAN

HarperTrophy®
An Imprint of HarperCollinsPublishers

Dedicated to the kids who inspired me at schools I visited in 1999...

In New Jersey: Moorestown Middle and South Valley in Moorestown, Harrison Township in Mullica Hill, Livingston Park in North Brunswick, Smalley in Bound Brook, Mountain Park in Berkeley Heights, Hamburg in Hamburg, Holly Glen in Williamstown, Davis in Camden, Oak Knoll in Summit, Hillview in Pompton Plains, Stonybrook in Kinnelon, Cedar Mountain in Vernon, Stephen Gerace and Pequannock Valley in Pequannock, Roland Rogers in Absecon, Durand in Vineland, Morgan in Sparta, St. Charles in Palmyra, Byram in Stanhope, Duffy and Mackinnon in Wharton, St. Charles Borromeo in Cinnaminson, Barley Sheaf in Flemington, Morris Plains in Morris Plains, St. Mathias in Somerset, Sharpe and Politz Foundation in Cherry Hill, Bacon in Millville, Indian Hill in Holmdel, Logan in Swedesboro, Cedar Hill in Towaco, Hillside in Bridgewater, Beeler and Van Zant in Marlton, Toms River Intermediate in Toms River, Allenwood in Allenwood, Delran Intermediate in Delran, Winslow #6 and Mullen in Sicklerville, Littlebrook in Princeton, Bernardsville Middle in Bernardsville.

In Pennsylvania: Lower Salford in Harleyville, Englewood, Knapp, and Gwynedd Square Schools in Lansdale, Hatfield in Hatfield, North Wales and Gwyn-Nor Schools in North Wales, Keith Valley in Horsham, Clarks Summit, Appletree, and Abington Heights Middle School in Wilkes-Barre, Quarry Hill in Yardley, Kutztown in Kutztown, March in Easton, Sugartown in Malvern, Penn Bernville in

Bernville, Jenkintown in Jenkintown.

In Texas: St. Mark's, Episcopal, Greenhill, and Parish Day School in Dallas. Redland Oaks, Coker, Northern Hills, Thousand Oaks, Northwood, Huebner, Oak Meadow, Stone Oak, and Longs Creek School in San Antonio. Roosevelt Alexander in Katy. Tomball Junior High in Tomball. Smith, Winship, Hirsch, Jenkins, and Dueitt School in Spring. Oak Creek, Beneke, Bammel, Ponderosa, Link, and Clark School in Houston.

In Oklahoma: Skyview, Central, Parkland, Ranchwood, Shedeck, Myers, Surrey Hills, Lakeview Middle, and Independence Middle School in Yukon. Central Middle, Mayfield Middle, Northridge, and Coronado School in Oklahoma City. Western Oaks in Bethany.

In New York: Goshen Intermediate in Goshen, Mt. Pleasant and Central Park School in Schenectady, Colton in Spring Valley, Murray Ave. in Larchmont.

In North Carolina: Sherwood Park, Vanstory Hills, Lillian Black, Hefner, and Brentwood School in Fayettville.

In Michigan: Warner, Bean, and Hanover Horton Middle in Spring Arbor.

Also: Hilliard Station in Hilliard, Ohio. Brunswick in Greenwich, Connecticut. The Right To Read Program in Presque Isle, Maine. And coolest of all, The Cairo American College in Egypt.

ACKNOWLEDGMENTS

Thanks to Loren James, cofounder of the Stuntmen's Association of Motion Pictures and Television

"Nobody ought ever to do that again."

—Annie Edson Taylor, the first person to
go over Niagara Falls and live, in 1901

JOHNNY HANGTIME

FALL IN NEW YORK

The Empire State Building points skyward, like a gigantic pencil, 1,454 feet over the island of Manhattan. It was built with sixty thousand tons of steel, I've been told. That's enough to lay down railroad tracks from New York to Baltimore. The building has 60 miles of water pipe and 3,500 miles of telephone wire. There are seventy-three elevators inside. On the outside, 6,500 windows need to be washed continually. The eighty-sixth floor observatory sits 1,050 feet above street level.

And I'm about to jump off it.

It's a clear day, just a few minutes after sunrise. New York City is spread out, waking up before me. I can look down on the Chrysler Building and the United Nations. There are three bridges in the distance stretching across the East River. The ships plowing through the early morning waters look like toys in a bathtub. The cars below don't look like Fords or Toyotas. They look like Hot Wheels and Matchbox. People—well, they're so tiny I can barely see them at all.

Looking out at the horizon, I estimate that visibility must be eighty miles or more. New Jersey lies across the Hudson River. I bet I can see all the way to Pennsylvania, Connecticut, and Massachusetts too. It occurs to me that alarm clocks must be going off up and down the East Coast right now. People are waking up groggily after a long night's sleep, putting their feet on solid ground.

Looking straight down past the tips of my sneakers, I can look down the eighty-six stories stretching toward Fifth Avenue below. The Empire State Building hasn't been the tallest building in the world for years, but it's still the most beautiful, if you ask me. I remember reading that they built the whole thing in just twenty-five weeks. Fourteen men were killed during the construction. But none of them *jumped* off.

I have been planning to do this for months. Thought about it over and over in my mind. I would wake up in the middle of the night thinking about it. Finally, I'm ready. I'm nervous. I'm scared. But I feel like King Kong.

They say a penny dropped from this height would go through a skull like a knife through Jell-O. What would happen to a human body that fell so far?

I would be killed, of course. No question about that. But would there be anything left of me? Any remains for Mom to identify? Or would some sanitation crew simply scrape me off the pavement like an egg off a skillet, and then continue on down the street picking up trash? If I think too much about that, I'll chicken out, I know.

The shadow of the sun is creeping across the city, one avenue at a time. The air is thin, and it's cold up here. Wind coming off the river makes the building sway back and forth slightly. Maybe it's just an optical illusion. I slide my sneakers forward a couple of inches, so the toes hang over the edge and my heels rest on brick.

My hands are behind my back, grasping the iron rails tightly. I can feel my heart beating. Maybe even hear it. Or is that a guy with a jackhammer fixing a pothole down below?

There's no turning back now. I bend my knees, let go of the iron bars, and push off, hard, stretching my arms out in front of me. For a moment, I feel like I'm suspended in the air, like a cartoon character who doesn't fall because he hasn't yet noticed he's run off a cliff.

And then, the inevitable. Gravity reaches up and grabs at me. I start to fall, first slowly. You pick up speed so fast in free fall. The wind rushes by my face, ripping at my hair. It turns me around. My clothes are flapping. It's dizzying.

I'm powerless now. It's out of my control. When you jump, it's the only time no part of your body is touching anything. There's nothing for your muscles to push against. It would be an incredibly relaxing experience, if only we *could* relax in this situation. Nobody can.

And it's over so quickly. In the movies, things like this go on forever. But real life doesn't happen in slo-mo.

It's over much more quickly than I expect. I don't have the chance to enjoy it. All too soon, my body hits bottom.

2

KIDS, DON'T TRY THIS AT HOME!

"**C**ut!" Roland Rivers hollered into his bullhorn. "That was beautiful, Johnny! Great job, everyone!"

Even before I landed in the middle of the air bag, I knew we had the shot. The crew gave me a nice round of applause. One of the guys helped me to my feet and into a window on the seventy-fourth floor. The rest of the crew deflated the air bag and removed the rigging from the side of the Empire State Building to get ready for the next scene they'd have to shoot.

I wiped the sweat off my forehead with my sleeve. Helicopters surrounding the building buzzed away.

There are only two kinds of people who jump off tall buildings: lunatics and stuntmen. I'm no lunatic.

My name is Johnny Thyme. That's what everybody calls me back home. But in the movie business I'm known by my "professional" name—Johnny Hangtime.

Stuntmen and stuntwomen, as you probably know, take the

place of actors and actresses when they have to shoot dangerous scenes for movies, TV, and commercials. Big stars aren't allowed to jump off buildings, crash through windows, run through fire—things like that. If they were to get hurt, it would ruin the whole movie and possibly their career. Most actors probably wouldn't do those dangerous stunts anyway. So professional stuntmen are hired to do the job.

Or stuntkids. I just turned thirteen. There are about seven hundred professional stunt people in the United States, but only a few of us are minors. So when child actors need to do something the least bit dangerous, there's a good chance I'll get the call to take their place.

The movie we were shooting was called *New York Nightmare*. It's about a group of terrorists who try to attract media attention to their political cause by committing terrible crimes at famous New York City landmarks. I was stunt doubling for the actor Ricky Corvette. He plays this brave kid who single-handedly stops the terrorists. It's a goofy story, but then, that's Hollywood. Not every movie can be *Gone with the Wind*, you know?

Roland Rivers is the director of *New York Nightmare*, and I trust him with my life. Roland is almost completely bald, but he has a long beard, and a ponytail sticks out the back of his head. He's got hair everywhere except where you're *supposed* to have it. Once I asked him why he has the ponytail and he replied in that great British accent of his, "Why, my good man, if I were to cut it off, I'd have no hair at all!"

We had the Empire State Building gag carefully worked out in advance, of course. That's what stunt people call a stunt—a gag. Roland and I spent days going over every detail so it would come off perfectly. He filmed my fall from several angles and distances. When

I hit the air bag, he shot it from a helicopter above the building.

The big air bag, you see, looks just like the surface of a blimp. The special-effects people will draw a blimp on a computer and paste it right into the scene. When Roland gets into the editing room, he will cut to a computer-generated long shot of a blimp hovering alongside the Empire State Building. When he splices all the fake shots together with the real shots of me, it will look like I jumped from the eighty-sixth floor observatory straight onto the blimp.

Roland could have faked the whole gag if he wanted to. Through careful camera placement, special effects, and by using background shots of New York, he could have filmed the scene in a Hollywood soundstage. That would have been a lot cheaper and safer, and most people watching the movie would never know the scene wasn't shot at the actual Empire State Building.

But Roland is a "stickler," as he puts it. He wants everything to look real.

"The audience must feel like they are *there*," he always says. "To make them feel that, *we* must be there. Do the thing. Put life on the line."

Both of us wanted to get the shot right the first time, and we did. If we had to shoot it all over again, it would cost a lot of money. Besides, jumping off the Empire State Building once was plenty for me.

"Did you *feel* them, Johnny?" Roland asked, throwing his arm around me as he ushered me into an office on the seventy-fourth floor.

"Uh, no," I replied, peeling off my kneepads and elbow pads. "Feel what?"

"Endorphins, baby! The endorphins!"

Oh, yeah. The endorphins.

Roland had been a high-school science teacher in England until he changed careers and got into directing movies. He says that chemicals called endorphins inhibit our brain cells from experiencing pain. When they get into our bloodstream and attach to certain nerve receptors, they put us in a state of euphoria. Roland believes that doing stunts like jumping out of buildings releases endorphins from the pituitary gland, which is about the size of a peanut and sits at the base of the skull. He thinks that if a scene gets *my* endorphins flowing, it will get the audience's endorphins flowing too.

Roland's kind of nutty, but he is a genius.

"You and I are the same, Johnny," Roland confided to me one day. "We need endorphins. You get them by doing stunts, I get them by watching you do stunts."

"It *was* exciting," I told Roland. I didn't want to disappoint him by letting him know I didn't feel any endorphins surging through my system.

"I wish I were you, Johnny," Roland sighed. "I'd be in a constant state of euphoria. But alas, I cannot. I lack but one quality that keeps me from achieving this unreachable goal."

"What's that, Roland?" I asked.

"Courage, my boy!" he bellowed. "Courage!" With that, he slapped me on the back and let out a cackling laugh.

At that moment, my mom burst into the office, ran toward me and wrapped her arms around me. Looking at her, you would think I had *missed* the air bag.

"Johnny!" she cried. "Are you okay? I'm sorry I was late. They closed off the observation deck and I couldn't convince the guard I was your mother."

"Everything went fine, Mom," I assured her. She started squeezing me and kissing me and stuff. The guys on the crew started making kissy faces and snickering behind Mom's back.

"Mrs. Thyme!" Roland boomed. "So good of you to stop by! Looking gorgeous, I might add. Johnny was fabulous, as always."

"Johnny," Mom begged, ignoring Roland. "I wish you would quit this. I'm going to have a heart attack one of these days."

"Quit?" Roland said, horrified. "Meredith, your son is a stunt *genius*! You must nurture this ability. He has a very unique and sought-after talent."

I had to laugh. As if jumping off a building takes talent! Mom turned to Roland and backed him into the corner, all serious.

"Was an ambulance waiting in case something went wrong, Roland?"

"Yes, Meredith," Roland said dutifully.

"Was the net in place in case Johnny missed the air bag?"

"Yes."

"Were there three doctors standing by at all times?"

"Yes."

"An EMS crew?"

"Yes! Meredith, every safety precaution was taken to protect your son, I assure you."

Mom appeared to relax a little, and Roland wrapped his arm gently around her shoulder.

"Meredith," he said softly. "Are you familiar with Galileo's law of falling bodies?"

Mom shook her head no. Roland has a way with words, and he started laying it on thick.

"All objects fall with a constant acceleration of thirty-two feet per second, Meredith. In other words, with each passing second, an object will fall thirty-two feet faster than it did the second before."

I knew Mom couldn't care less, but Roland could just grab people with his eyes and rivet their attention on him. He was a master at it.

"It doesn't matter if you drop an anvil or a tennis ball," Roland continued. "Heavy objects don't fall any faster than light ones. You don't believe me, do you? Hold out your hands."

Roland picked up two statues of the Empire State Building from a shelf. One was about two inches tall and the other was the size of a large bowling trophy. He placed one statue in each of Mom's palms, caressing her hands from beneath.

"Now, drop them!"

Mom dropped the two statues. Sure enough, they both hit the floor at the exact same instant. A security guard looked at Roland suspiciously.

"See?" Roland cooed, still holding Mom's hands. "Because of the law of falling bodies, I knew Johnny would fall sixteen feet in the first second. And I knew he would fall forty-eight feet the next second. And I knew he would fall eighty feet the third second. So after three seconds, Johnny was moving ninety-six feet per second, sixty-five miles per hour, and he had fallen one hundred forty-four feet. That's the height of a twelve-story building. And do you know where we put that big, soft air bag Johnny landed on, Meredith?"

"Twelve stories down?" Mom asked.

"Precisely!" Roland exclaimed. "Johnny was in good hands—the hands of Galileo. The hands of Aristotle. The hands of Isaac Newton, and the hands of America's own Albert Einstein!"

As far as *I'm* concerned, Galileo, Aristotle, Newton, and Einstein didn't know squat about falling objects. None of *them* ever jumped off a building. But it was a masterful performance on Roland's part, I had to admit. Like I said, the man is a genius.

Roland and I have made six movies together since I started doing stunt work three years ago. He's become sort of like a dad to me. We work really well together, and now I'm his personal stunt-kid. He's had me thrown down flights of stairs, through windows, out of cars, and off horses, but I haven't broken a single bone in my body.

Well, that's not exactly true. I broke a bone in my foot once. But it was because I wasn't paying attention and fell off a curb.

"Meredith," Roland said sweetly, "may I have the honor of your company for dinner this evening?"

Roland says he's a confirmed bachelor who is married to his work, but he has been asking my mom to go out on a date with him ever since he met her. So far, she has refused.

"I'm busy, Roland."

"Perhaps tomorrow, then?"

"Roland, I'll make a deal with you. I'll go out with you when you give me my Johnny back and make a *serious* film—no stunts."

Mom likes what she calls "art films"—these awful foreign movies where nothing happens and you have to read subtitles with the characters whining about how miserable they are. Her favorite movie of all time is *My Dinner With Andre*.

I watched it with her once. These two guys sit in a restaurant eating dinner and talking for two hours. That's *all* they do! I would tell you what they talked about, but I fell asleep after five minutes.

"You present me with a dilemma, Meredith," Roland said as he rubbed his beard. "I can either have the company of a beautiful woman or the talent of her son who is making me a rich man."

"But not both," Mom said.

"For now, I must bid you *adieu*," Roland said, finally releasing each of Mom's hands with a kiss. "Johnny, I will meet you at Liberty Island. Bonjour!"

"The guy's not even French," Mom snorted when Roland was out of earshot.

Late that night, in our hotel room, Mom asked me again if I would give up stunt work. I said no. I want to please her, of course. But stunting is my life. It's what I do. Maybe for me, it's like an addiction.

"What will it take to make you stop?" she asked.

"I don't know," I replied. "I don't know."

3

CRAZY JOE THYME

Mom is what you'd call an overprotective single parent. Well, that's not really fair. I mean, how many moms have to deal with a son who would willingly jump off the Empire State Building? But even when I was a little kid, her favorite expression was "Be careful."

Be careful to chew your food well or you'll choke. Be careful to wash your hands or you'll get germs. Be careful stepping off that escalator. Be careful not to talk to strangers. Be careful of everything.

I get tired of hearing it after a while. Sometimes I just don't *want* to be careful. Sometimes I just want to cut loose. Maybe that's part of the reason why I got into doing stunts in the first place.

Mom begs me to stop stunting just about every day. But she has never *insisted* that I stop. So I keep doing it. Besides, I know we need the money.

Stuntmen are paid by the gag. The more dangerous the gag, the more you get paid. It can range from $25 for a simple stunt all the way up to thousands of dollars.

For instance, once I had to do a stair fall. That's when you fall down a flight of stairs. It was simple. I wore lots of padding under my clothes, on my elbows, knees, ribs, and behind. The stairs were carpeted, and I didn't get hurt. I was paid $100. It would have been $150 if it had been metal stairs with no carpet, because that's more dangerous.

Roland messed up the first take and we had to shoot the stair fall again. So I got paid *another* $100. As it turned out, Roland kept having trouble with the scene, and he insisted on shooting it over and over again. So I fell down the stairs a dozen times that day and earned $1,200. It was a great day.

Sure beats getting a paper route, I'll say that much.

Anyway, I give all the money I earn to Mom. She's a secretary and doesn't get paid much. My dad died three years ago, and he didn't leave us anything. In fact, after he died, Mom had to pay off his debts. Dad didn't have any insurance. He said he didn't believe in it.

I wasn't going to bring up my dad, but I guess I just did. This is as good a place as any to tell you about him.

My dad, Joe Thyme, was crazy. Or so people say anyway. I was only ten when he died, so my memories of him are of things we did together when I was little. But people have told me stories.

Dad grew up on a ranch in Texas, and he was so sure he was going to become a famous Hollywood actor that he dropped out of high school and moved to California. As it turned out, he was a terrible actor. He took a job as a grip, which is a guy who carries stuff around on a movie set.

One day, he was working on a western and the director needed a guy to get shot and fall off a horse. They didn't have enough stuntmen.

Dad had grown up with horses his whole life and loved horses, so he volunteered.

"I been fallin' off horses since before I could walk," he claimed.

He did the stunt, and everybody saw that while Dad couldn't act, he was great at falling off a horse. He told me, in fact, that throwing his body around was the only thing he was *ever* good at. The next thing you know, Dad was a professional stuntman.

He met my mom around the same time. Mom says she has a thing for unusual men. The two of them fell in love, got married, and had me.

Soon Dad was getting punched, kicked, set on fire, thrown through windows—all the usual gags. I remember he would come home at night and soak in a hot bath for an hour to ease his aches and pains before dinner.

I've been told my dad would do *anything*. If they needed a guy to get run over by a truck, he would volunteer. If they needed somebody to get shot, he would be the first in line. If one of the other stuntmen said a gag was too dangerous and refused to do it, Dad would take it on. He had a reputation in the industry for being fearless and a little crazy. People used to say my dad was indestructable.

So I guess doing stunts is in my genes. I remember when I was a very little boy I used to look out the second-floor window of our house and think about jumping out. There was a concrete sidewalk below the window, so it was too dangerous.

But then, one day, some workmen were fixing the streets. They parked a dump truck with a big pile of sand in it right outside my house. When I looked out the window and saw it, I couldn't resist. I climbed up on my windowsill and jumped out.

Mom and Dad were downstairs. Mom caught a glimpse of my body dropping into the truck and totally freaked out. She came rushing outside, where she found me dusting the sand off my pants. Mom was furious and warned me never to do anything like that again. But Dad had one of those secret "That's my boy!" looks on his face.

When Mom wasn't around, Dad and I used to have these crazy contests. Dad would jump off a ladder, and I would jump off a moving bicycle. Then I would jump off the roof of the car, and Dad would jump off the garage. I would climb a tree and jump off a branch, and Dad would top it in some way.

"Be a man!" Dad would taunt me. "If you were a *real* man you could do it."

Dad was bigger and stronger than me, naturally. I never beat him, though I kept trying.

Mom used to come home from work and ask me what I did after school.

"I jumped off the fence," I'd say.

"Why did you jump off the fence?"

"Because Dad did."

"If Dad jumped off the Brooklyn Bridge, would you do that too?"

Mom and I stopped, looked at each other, and laughed. One time, for a movie, Dad *did* jump off the Brooklyn Bridge.

Every so often, Dad would take me with him on a movie set so I could see what he did for a living. People always gathered around and asked, "Are you going to be a stuntman like your daddy when you grow up?"

I didn't get into stunting until after Dad died. That happened when I was ten. Dad was shooting an adventure movie at Niagara Falls, and he took me along. They needed a stuntman to drive a motorboat over the falls.

It wasn't any ordinary boat. At the push of a button, wings

popped out of the boat and it was converted into a plane. Instead of plummeting over the edge of the falls, the script called for the boat to sprout wings and fly away. It was pretty cool.

All the other stuntmen on the set turned down the gag. Dad had a pilot's license and he, of course, accepted the job.

Everything went smoothly except for one thing—the wings never popped out of the boat.

I never had the chance to say good-bye to him. I watched as Dad plummeted over Niagara Falls. It was horrifying.

Ever since the accident, Mom hasn't mentioned Dad in front of me. If I bring him up, she changes the subject. There are no pictures of him around the house, none of his awards or trophies to remind us of him. I guess the memory would be too painful for Mom.

Pieces of the boat were found all over the Niagara River after the accident. A week later, the clothes Dad had been wearing were found stuck on a rock outcropping several miles downstream. His body was never recovered.

Every so often a rumor pops up that Joe Thyme is still alive, but I try to ignore it. It's like sightings of Elvis Presley. People just don't want their heroes to die.

4

LIBERTY . . . OR DEATH

"Okay, Johnny, we're ready for you," Roland bellowed through his bullhorn. "This is the Big Girl scene, everybody. Take one. Roll camera!"

Picture this: I'm standing on the Statue of Liberty's head. You read that right. Lady Liberty. One of the largest statues in the world, the grand old symbol that welcomed to America millions of tired, poor, huddled masses yearning to breathe free. I doubt that any of them were yearning to climb inside the statue's head to defuse a bomb planted in there, but that's what I have to do for this scene.

You see, in *New York Nightmare*, these terrorists find out that the copper skin of Liberty appears to be strong but is actually quite thin and light. It *had* to be. The statue was designed and built in France. It needed to be taken apart, shipped to America by boat, and reassembled like a gigantic jigsaw puzzle.

The leader of the terrorists tells his comrades that the Statue of Liberty is just an iron skeleton covered by 350 copper plates, each the thickness of a silver dollar. The whole thing is held together by rivets. The head was constructed separately from the rest of her body, so the neck is a weak point. One good blast would blow Liberty's head right off.

These terrorists (I had gotten to know the actors playing them and they were actually very nice guys) plant a powerful explosive inside Liberty's head so they can blow the symbol of America to smithereens. And here's the kicker: They decide to blow up Liberty on the Fourth of July, right in the middle of the fireworks!

"If *that* doesn't get us on the news, what will?" the leader of the terrorists asks his buddies.

It's a stupid plot, I know. I don't write these scripts, I just do as I'm told.

The wind was whipping up off New York Harbor, and I waited for it to settle down before doing the gag. The hardest part about being a stuntkid is the waiting. Once I'm ready to begin, I'm able to wipe everything else out of my mind and focus on what I have to do. But as I stand there waiting I start thinking, "Am I crazy? Have I totally lost it? What am I doing up here?"

Roland was starting to lose his patience, but he knew that in a situation this dangerous you don't want to take any chances.

"Johnny!" Roland finally hollered. "As you Americans say, 'Give me liberty or give me death!' But give it to me before tomorrow!"

Roland and I had gone over the script line by line. We had already shot the scene where I climbed down a rope ladder from a helicopter onto Liberty's head. My job now was to climb inside a window on her crown, grab the bomb, climb back out on the crown, and fling the bomb as far as I could into New York Harbor.

The fireworks would be edited in later, but a half a second after

I let the bomb go, the pyrotechnic crew would set off a bright orange explosion. Then Roland will cut to some ordinary kids watching the Fourth of July fireworks. They think the explosion is part of the show, and they *ooh* and *ahh* over it. They never realize that a national catastrophe has been narrowly averted.

Naturally, the statue will be unharmed, but the force of the explosion is supposed to knock me off the crown and onto Liberty Island.

The wind was beginning to die down. I paused to take a deep breath before the gag. What a view you get from up there! It was dark outside, but I could see, in the distance, the Brooklyn and Verrazano bridges, and the lights of lower Manhattan. I wasn't nearly as high as I had been for the Empire State Building gag, but being surrounded on all sides by water made it feel more treacherous.

Liberty was flooded with lights, and as I looked down, I got a view of her that very few people have ever seen. Her head was about ten feet across, but I had to be careful not to wander too close to the edge or I'd fall off—right into those massive hands. Each one must have been sixteen feet long. Her fingers alone looked to be twice as tall as I am.

Roland signaled me again, so I figured I'd better stop sightseeing and do the gag.

"Meet you at Pizza Hut!" I shouted to Roland.

That's a little superstition Roland and I have. Before one of the first stunts I ever did, I was nervous and Roland tried to relax me by saying he'd take me out for pizza as soon as we were finished. Ever since then, one of us usually says, "Meet you at Pizza Hut!"—or some other fast food joint—before each gag.

I got down on my hands and knees and eased myself backward

into the window of the crown. I grabbed the fake bomb and climbed back out the window.

There are seven spikes sticking out of Liberty's crown. Roland, who knows just about *everything* about *everything*, told me they represent the seven continents and seven seas. The script called for me to climb out on the spike directly above Liberty's right eye and heave the bomb off. That's what I did.

The blast set off by the pyrotechnic guys was bigger than I thought it would be. I could feel the heat from the explosion. It made me stagger back a bit, which was fine because it would make the scene look more realistic. Next, I had to fall.

The Statue of Liberty is 151 feet high from toe to torch. Her head is lower than the torch, so it's about a 100-foot drop from the crown. Then there's the base of the statue, which is 65 feet high itself. So I was looking at a 165-foot free fall. No helmet. No parachute. No bungee cord. No hidden wires. No nothing.

Falling 165 feet isn't such a difficult fall, really. I've done it plenty of times. It's over before you know it. Falling 300 feet is far. When you're about to make a 300-foot fall, that's when you wonder if you've seen your last sunset, eaten your last meal, hugged your mom for the last time.

In the stunt world, we call a fall a *bump* or a *brodie*. Apparently, there was this nut named Steve Brodie who jumped off a bridge back in the 1880s. I don't know if he survived or not. After that, jumping from a high place came to be called "pulling a Brodie."

Anybody can pull a Brodie. It's doing it without getting killed that's the hard part. And as we stunt guys say, the difference between *killed* and *skilled* is just one letter.

Just like with the Empire State Building gag, we used an air bag to cushion my landing. The type of bag we used on Liberty Island is made of nylon and about the size of a large swimming pool. There are vents called *breathers* on the sides. When you hit the bag, air is forced out the breathers so the stuntman doesn't get hurt.

That is, if you *hit* the air bag. If you miss it by a foot, you could break every bone in your body. Naturally, you've got to aim for the center of the bag. You do that the instant you jump. Human beings aren't like cats. We're not very good at mid-course corrections.

It's important to learn how to land correctly. You can't land feet first, because the impact will snap the large bones in your legs like twigs, or drive them into your pelvis. Also, if you land on your feet and bend your knees, there's a good chance your knees are going to come up and smash you in the face, which is no fun at all.

For a front fall, the trick is to keep your head down and eyes on the landing spot. At the last instant, you pull your head up and spread your body out.

You never want to fall with a forward somersault, because you might break your neck. Rolling on one shoulder is okay. This is called a stunt roll. It spreads the impact across your whole body instead of putting it all on one part.

But the script called for me to do a back fall. This is harder than a front fall because you can't see the air bag. You have to trust your instincts.

I staggered back off Liberty's spiked crown and gave a little push with my toe to clear the statue. All was silent, but within a second the rush of air roared in my ears. I felt myself tilting a little too far backward, which is dangerous. I didn't want to land on my head. By bringing my hands down closer to my legs, I shifted my center of gravity and kept my body nearly horizontal. That's how I landed, spread-eagled in the middle of the bag with a *whoosh*.

"Cut!" Roland yelled. "Beautiful! Don't move a muscle, Johnny! Not one muscle!"

5

THE GREAT RICKY CORVETTE

I didn't move a muscle, just as Roland instructed. There was a smattering of polite applause from the crew. I lay on my back waiting for further instructions from Roland. My mom, I knew, was breathing a sigh of relief.

"Where's Ricky?" boomed Roland. "Will somebody get Ricky out here?"

Everybody started nervously running around, as if they'd heard there was a hurricane approaching.

"Get Ricky!" everybody was muttering.

"Where *is* he?" one of the grips asked.

"He'll be here any second!" the makeup girl said.

"He's coming!" Roland's assistant said excitedly.

"He's *here*!" somebody else exclaimed.

Finally, an enormous yacht pulled up to the edge of Liberty Island. On the back was one word, painted in two-foot-high letters: RICKY. The yacht was secured to a dock and the door opened. Two big, burly guys with walkie-talkies came out and looked around, like they were checking to see if it was safe. One of them nodded, and the great Ricky Corvette emerged from the yacht.

Ricky Corvette is the fourteen-year-old star of movies like *Skate Fever, Nightmare in Los Angeles,* and *The Kid Who Ran for President*. His most recent film—*Virtually Perfect*—grossed over $200 million. Last year, *Entertainment Weekly* listed him as one of the ten most powerful people in Hollywood.

He lives in a Malibu mansion with his mother and all kinds of bodyguards and gardeners and other hangers-on. He hardly ever goes out in public, and when he goes anywhere, the paparazzi trail him like bloodhounds.

The public thinks Ricky Corvette is the All-American boy. All-American *jerk* is more like it. Ricky Corvette! He's so cute he makes me want to throw up.

Oh, I'm sure that's not his real name. That's his movie-star name. His real name is probably Ricky Dufus or Ricky Dorkus or something. I'm sure he changed his name to Corvette because he thought it would sound cool. Nobody will ever know, because Ricky's personal life is top secret.

Ricky stepped off the yacht and looked up at the Statue of Liberty.

"Nice lookin' babe," he said in that sickeningly adorable voice of his. Everybody laughed. If you're famous enough, I guess, people will laugh at even the dumbest lines.

He was dressed just like me, in blue jeans and a leather jacket. His jet black hair had been perfectly arranged. I think he had enough grease in there to lube a Greyhound bus. He was wearing sunglasses, so nobody could see his famous blue eyes—the eyes that every teenage girl in America dreams about when they go to sleep at night. He looked like a young Elvis Presley.

Everybody stopped what they were doing and watched him. I overheard one of the female members of the crew comment on how gorgeous Ricky was. He was followed off the yacht by the two most important people in his life—his mother and his agent. Not necessarily in that order.

Ricky sauntered over to the set like he was expecting everybody to break into applause at his mere presence. He probably expects a standing ovation when he goes to the bathroom.

"Ricky," Roland said, "do you know your lines? Do you need a glass of water or anything?" Roland hadn't offered *me* a glass of water, I noticed, and *I* fell off the Statue of Liberty.

"He doesn't need water," Ricky's agent said gruffly. "He needs another million bucks or he's off this picture."

"What's the matter, Ricky?" Roland asked.

"Hey, man," Ricky grumbled. "My contract calls for a gallon of M&Ms in my yacht."

"They weren't there?"

"No," the agent interrupted. "A gallon of Reese's *Pieces* were there. When Ricky Corvette says he wants M&Ms, he doesn't want Reese's Pieces. He doesn't want Skittles. He wants M&Ms!"

Roland rolled his eyes. "Reese's Pieces were good enough for E.T.," he said.

"Well they're not good enough for R.C.," the agent barked.

Ricky is either an egomaniac or a chocoholic. Maybe both. His mother jumped in between Roland and the agent. "It's not that Ricky is being difficult," she explained. "But he's under strict orders from his nutritionist—"

"We'll get Ricky some M&Ms as soon as this scene is done," Roland snapped, obviously irritated. "Now let's set up the shot, everybody!"

Reluctantly, Ricky knelt on the grass next to the air bag. It was important that he copy the exact position in which I was lying, so it would look like *Ricky* had taken the fall off the Statue of Liberty.

"Oh man, this grass is *wet*!" Ricky complained, getting back on his feet.

"Ricky says the grass is wet!" screamed Roland's assistant into a walkie-talkie.

"The grass is wet!" somebody at the other side of the set responded.

"Dry the grass!" everybody started yelling.

Somebody rushed over with a hair dryer and pointed it at the grass for a few minutes. While he was waiting for the grass to dry, Ricky pulled out a pocket mirror and looked at himself. When he was convinced that he wouldn't get his pants wet, he lay down in the grass. A makeup girl dashed over and put some powder on his forehead.

"Hey!" Ricky warned her. "Sweetheart, you mess up my hair and you'll be waiting tables at McDonald's tomorrow!"

Man, I thought. Ricky's so out of touch, he thinks they have waitresses at McDonald's! He probably has a private chef cook all his meals for him, a food taster to make sure the food isn't poisoned, and a second food taster to make sure the first food taster doesn't poison the food.

Finally, when Ricky was in the right position, Roland gave me the okay to get up. Mom dashed over and hugged me.

"Okay, quiet everybody!" boomed Roland. "Roll camera!"

"Ohhhhhhhhhh!" moaned Ricky. "My leg!"

"Cut!" Roland said. "That was great, Ricky!"

Great? I had jumped off the Empire State Building and fallen off the Statue of Liberty. All Ricky Corvette did was say, "Oh, my leg." Still, everybody erupted into a standing ovation, as if the president had just finished delivering his State of the Union address. Sometimes life isn't fair.

I hated Ricky Corvette the minute I met him three years ago. I remember we were introduced when I was his stunt double on *Skate Fever*. It was my first job. I stuck out my hand to shake, and he looked at it like I was going to give him cooties. "You *do* look a little like me," he said, "but not as good-looking."

Ricky won't even call me by my name. He always refers to me as "the stunt kid." "Let the stuntkid do it," he always says whenever there's a scene that doesn't show his face. "Hey, stuntkid! Get me a Coke." What a dirtbag.

My work was finished for the day, but I asked Mom if we could hang around. Roland was going to shoot the last scene of *New York Nightmare*, and I really wanted to see it.

6

AUGUSTA

A yacht almost as big as Ricky Corvette's yacht pulled up to the Liberty Island dock. On the back was the word AUGUSTA. We had been waiting for it, and Roland was getting more and more angry that it was late. After a few anxious minutes, out stepped Augusta Wind.

That's not her real name, of course. It *couldn't* be. Could it? Augusta Wind? Come on! Who would name their daughter Augusta, especially when their last name is Wind? Augusta Wind had to be her stage name, her modeling name.

When she stepped off the yacht, there was an audible, involuntary gasp from all the guys on the crew. Augusta Wind was, without a doubt, the most beautiful teenage girl on the face of the earth. Check that. The galaxy. The universe. Not that I've seen them all, but I can't imagine any girl who looked as gorgeous as Augusta Wind.

She was wearing a flowing white dress that whipped around her in the breeze. Her long brown hair was flying all over, but not like it does with normal people. When Augusta gave her head a little shake, her hair flowed the way it does in those countless shampoo commercials I've seen her in. Like it's in slow motion.

Augusta has a multimillion-dollar contract with Cover Girl, and all she has to do for it is wash her hair, put on makeup, and smile for the camera. Nice life.

She was so perfect in every way, it was hard to believe she was a person. She almost didn't look real. Augusta just stood there on the dock, expressionless.

A middle-aged woman wearing about a dozen bracelets, necklaces, and earrings hopped off the yacht. She pushed past Augusta and rushed over to Roland. I guessed she was Augusta's mother.

"Sorry we're late!" she bubbled. "We thought we were supposed to go to the Liberty Bell."

"The Liberty Bell?" Roland said through clenched teeth. "Ma'am, the title of this film is *New York Nightmare*. I spent my whole life in England, but even *I* know the Liberty Bell is in Philadelphia. Did you think Ricky was going to fall off the Liberty Bell?"

"It didn't make sense to me either," Augusta's mother said. "That's why we turned around."

Man, if *my* mom had confused the Statue of Liberty with the Liberty Bell, I think I would have *died*. But Augusta was still expressionless. She didn't say a word. She must be one of those really dumb fashion models, I figured. She probably can't say anything unless it's written down for her.

Augusta's mom and Ricky's mom embraced like old friends. Augusta and Ricky didn't exactly leap into each other's arms, but everybody knows they're an "item." You can't pick up a newspaper or magazine without seeing a picture of them at some exclusive nightclub or private party. They'll get married as soon as they legally can, I imagine.

Augusta must be a real jerk. Who else but a real jerk would fall for a real jerk like Ricky Corvette?

"Places, everybody!" Roland shouted. "We're behind schedule." Roland pronounces *schedule* like "shed-jull." that always cracks me up.

Augusta knelt down carefully in front of Ricky, who was still on the ground after his "fall" from the Statue of Liberty.

"Okay, Ricky," Roland instructed. "Let's pick it up from the last line." I pulled out my script and found the right page. . . .

The force of the explosion blows Ricky off Liberty's crown and he plummets to the ground as the fireworks explode all around him.

SLICK
(moaning)
Ohhhhhhhh, my leg!

REBECCA
(crouching over him)
It's just a flesh wound, my darling.
You'll be back in school on Monday.

SLICK
(grimacing)
I hope so. This weekend has been
almost as dangerous as riding
the subway.

REBECCA
(laughs)
You saved New York . . . again.

SLICK
(modestly)
It was nothing, Becky.
Anybody could have done it.

REBECCA
(taking his hand)
But *you* did it, Slick.
New York loves you.
And I love you.

SLICK
I love New York.
And I love *you*.

They move their heads together slowly and kiss
passionately. The kiss lasts five seconds, time enough
for flag waving and the finale of the fireworks show to be
superimposed over their faces.

FADE OUT

It was uncomfortable to watch Ricky and Augusta kissing, but
irresistible at the same time. I've never kissed a girl. Not like that,
anyway. I certainly wouldn't want to do it with fifty people standing
around watching. With a girl as beautiful as Augusta, though, I might
make an exception.

"Cut!" Roland shouted. "Lovely. Nice work, everyone. I will be in
touch if we have to do any reshoots or dubbing."

The crew gave Ricky and Augusta a standing ovation. Augusta

got up without a word and left with her mom.

People who never say anything fascinate me. Are they so quiet because they're snobby? Because they have nothing to say? Because they're angry? Because they don't have a thought in their head? You never know. I wondered about Augusta Wind.

Ricky Corvette's agent stayed to argue with Roland for a while, so Ricky couldn't leave right away. A few of the guys on the crew asked him for autographs for their kids. He turned them down.

It had been a long day and I was tired. Roland had rented a ferry to take everybody back to Manhattan. It was parked alongside Ricky Corvette's yacht.

On the way to the dock, Mom and I found ourselves walking alongside Ricky's mom. We didn't have anything to say to one another, and it quickly became awkward. Finally, Ricky's mom felt she had to break the ice.

"It must be difficult," she said, "falling in the dirt all the time, getting your clothes soiled, and so forth."

"It's not so bad," I replied.

"It's difficult for *me*," Mom said, mussing up my hair. "I have to watch. Johnny *likes* it."

"Well, I want you to know I think it's just dear that your son does the stunts for my son's films."

She said *dear* like I was her pet.

"Well," Mom replied, "It's just dear of your son to do the dialogue for my son's films."

Ricky's mom looked at my mom as if she had been insulted. Then she walked away in a huff and climbed aboard her yacht.

7

BORIS BONNER

We wrapped up *New York Nightmare* at the end of August. The studio was thrilled, because Roland finished the movie on time and under budget. Mom was thrilled because I came away with just a few bumps and bruises.

Mom and I stayed in New York for a few days so I could see the sights of the city without having to jump off them. Also, Ricky Corvette's lawyer asked me and Mom to stop by his office before we went back to California.

The law offices of Pazan, Rothman, and Gavin were really fancy. I didn't even want to sit on the chairs in the waiting room, because they looked like they belonged in a museum or something.

After a few minutes, Mom and I were ushered into Barry Rothman's office. There were pictures of Ricky Corvette all over the walls. Barry Rothman was a big man with silvery hair. While he shook my hand and asked me how the movie went, I wondered why he really wanted to see me.

"Johnny, you've been doing Ricky Corvette's stunts for three years now," he finally said. "I'd like to go over a few things in your contract, if you're agreeable."

"We'll look it over," Mom said. She had on her serious, don't-mess-with-us face.

My contract with Ricky Corvette specified certain "dangerous" activities I wasn't allowed to do in my spare time. For instance, I couldn't go bungee jumping or snowboarding. The reason was that if I were to get injured and put out of action, I wouldn't be able to take Ricky's place in a movie, and it would damage his career. So my contract had a long list of activities I wasn't allowed to participate in. . . .

Parachuting. Firing a gun or shooting a bow and arrow. I wasn't allowed to go to dances or rock concerts, because somebody might jump off the stage and land on me. I wasn't allowed to be within ten yards of a trampoline for the same reason. I couldn't take gym class at school. I couldn't go mountain climbing.

Most important, fighting was strictly prohibited. If I got into a fight with anybody, my contract with Ricky Corvette would be terminated immediately.

"Just a few more things," the lawyer said, handing me and Mom a sheet of paper.

The paper said that from now on I was required to wear a seat belt any time I was in a moving vehicle. No problem, I do that anyway. It also said I would need to get written permission from Ricky's lawyer before I traveled by helicopter or airplane. Fair enough. Finally, it said I was not allowed to go on escalators, motorcycles, minibikes, wooden bridges, rope bridges, seesaws, monkey bars, or swings.

"I know it's kind of silly," the lawyer chuckled as he handed me a pen. "But it's for your own protection, Johnny. You can never be too safe."

"Are you sure you want to sign that?" Mom asked. "I mean, you won't even be able to go on an *escalator* anymore."

"I'll take the stairs, Mom," I said, as I signed the contract and handed it to her to co-sign.

Then it was back to California and back to school. I was excited about starting eighth grade in September.

I'm sure Ricky Corvette and Augusta Wind have private tutors, but I've always attended public school. We don't have the money for private school or private tutors. I do my stunts on weekends, vacations, and sometimes after school. Every so often, I get to take a day off from school to do a stunt.

On the first day of English class, as always, everybody had to write a composition about what they did over summer vacation.

HOW I SPENT MY SUMMER VACATION
by Johnny Thyme

This summer I went to New York City, where I jumped off the Empire State Building, was blown off the Statue of Liberty by a bomb, was hit by a bus, fell off a subway train, was set on fire, and was chased through Times Square by terrorists armed with assault rifles. I killed ten of them in Central Park with a hand grenade, and saved the city from nuclear annihilation.

That's what I would have *liked* to write. But I couldn't. Too bad too, because it would have really blown the rest of the class away.

The problem is, my contract with Ricky Corvette *also* states very clearly that I'm not allowed to *tell* anybody I'm a stuntkid.

Ricky, like a lot of movie stars, wants the public to believe *he* does all the dangerous stuff in his movies *himself*. He needs it to protect his image, I suppose.

If the public ever found out that all Ricky Corvette did was lie on the ground and moan, "Oh, my leg!" people might stop going to see his movies. His career would be over. And if anybody found out that *I* was the one who spilled the beans, I'd never get to do another stunt for Ricky again.

So I have to keep my mouth shut. Only me and Mom know the truth, plus some people in the movie industry. There is always a "closed set" on Ricky's movies, so word doesn't get around that he doesn't actually do any stunts. The general public thinks Ricky Corvette is a rough, tough "action hero."

What a joke! In reality, Ricky Corvette is such a wimp that he's afraid to cross the street without his mommy. And he's such a klutz, he can barely walk without tripping over his own feet.

I was at my locker, at the end of that first day of school, when I noticed a kid staring at me from a few lockers away. I didn't look up.

"Hey kid," the kid asked, "what's your name?"

"Johnny Thyme."

He was a big kid, bigger than me. He must have been new to school. I didn't recognize him. He had a crew cut and was wearing a heavy-metal T-shirt. He stuck out his hand for me to shake and I stuck out mine.

"Boris Bonner," he said. "Nice to meet ya."

As he said it, Boris tightened his grip on my hand. I tried to pull away, but he held on tight. Then he began squeezing.

I didn't want to let him know it hurt. I squeezed back, but it was clear that he was stronger than me. Boris looked into my eyes, searching for fear. I fought to pretend he wasn't hurting me. He was crushing the bones of my knuckles together. I thought about shouting or kicking him, but that would have been admitting defeat.

Just as the pain was becoming unbearable, he released my hand.

"So Johnny Thyme," Boris said with a grin, "how come you weren't in gym with the rest of the class?"

"I have asthma," I lied. I couldn't tell him my contract with Ricky Corvette prohibited me from taking gym class.

"Bummer," Boris Bonner muttered. He was about to walk away, but then he came back and put his face about a foot from mine. He had bad breath. "Hey, Thyme. You got a dollar on you?"

I had a couple of dollars in my pocket, but I didn't particularly want to give one to Boris Bonner. Then again, I didn't particularly want to turn him down either. He looked like the kind of kid who wanted to start a fight for the stupidest reason. And the last thing I needed was to get in a fight.

Maybe he just wants to *borrow* a dollar, I figured. He didn't *say* that, but maybe that's what he meant. He'll give me the dollar back tomorrow. By just giving him a lousy buck, I figured, I would get him out of my face. I pulled a bill out of my pocket and handed it to him.

"That's a good boy," he said, and walked down the hall. Right away, I wished I hadn't given him the dollar.

Back when I was ten, keeping my stunt work to myself wasn't a big deal. Nobody ever asked what I did after school or on weekends, and I didn't tell. If a kid invited me over to his house to play and

I had to shoot a movie that day, I just told him I had a dentist appointment or had to visit a relative or something.

In the last couple of years, though, things have changed. Kids notice everything now. This really pretty girl in my class invited me to a school dance last year. I couldn't tell her that I wasn't allowed to go to dances. After I turned her down with some lame excuse, I guess she told everybody, because the next day, a lot of kids looked at me like I was weird.

It has made things difficult for me. When a group of guys would pick up a football at recess and start throwing it around, I'd pretend I didn't see them so they wouldn't invite me to play. When kids would gather in the playground before school and start talking about what they were going to do over the weekend, I couldn't tell them the truth—that I would be having a fistfight on top of a speeding train, for instance. I'd say I had to visit my grandmother, or some other boring thing I wouldn't actually be doing. Kids must have thought I was boring too. I suppose that's why I pretty much stayed by myself.

I'm proud of my stunt work. I wish I could brag about it. But sometimes I regret that I ever got started stunting in the first place.

8

TIME OF MY LIFE

I was ten when it all started. Dad had just had the accident at Niagara Falls and I was going out of my mind at home. I had always been a daredevil, but Dad was always around to supervise me. When Mom caught me jumping off the garage one day, she was pretty upset. I could understand it. She had just lost her husband and she didn't want anything to happen to me.

Mom suggested I take up gymnastics. I guess she thought that if I got into a sport, I might get some of that energy out of my system. Maybe I wouldn't follow in Dad's footsteps.

I had seen gymnastics on TV during the Olympics, and it looked pretty cool. I gave it a try for a month or so. But somehow, vaulting off a pommel horse didn't give me the same rush that I got from vaulting off the garage. It just didn't make my endorphins kick in, I guess.

Mom tried to get me interested in team sports after that, but I never really liked them. I mean, look at baseball. The national pastime, they call it. What a lame game. You wait like an hour between pitches for something to happen while everybody stands around spitting and scratching themselves.

Most sports are the same, it seems to me. They're just a simulation of warfare—two teams trying to push their opponents across a battlefield and score a goal on them. Soccer—run up and down a field kicking a ball. Hockey—skate up and down a rink pushing a puck. Basketball—run up and down a court dribbling a ball. Football—run up and down a field knocking each other over. They were all the same as far as I was concerned, and I just wasn't into them.

"How about bowling?" Mom asked one day when I was moping around after school. "You don't run up and down a field in bowling."

"Bowling?" I asked, incredulously. "That has got to be the all-time most boring sport in the world, Mom! You roll a ball down an alley to knock down pins. Snooze! I mean, if you could lie on a skateboard and roll down the alley to see how many pins you could knock down with your *head*, *that* would be cool."

Mom looked at me with the worried expression she always gets when I remind her of Dad. A few weeks later, she made me go see a "counselor."

That's what she called him. I'm sure she was afraid that if she used the word *psychologist*, I might weird out. To Mom's generation, I think, going to see a psychologist meant you must be crazy or something is horribly wrong with you. These days, lots of kids see them and everybody's pretty cool about it. Going to a shrink didn't bother me at all.

Mom couldn't really afford the psychologist, but she thought it was important to figure out why I had this compulsion to do dangerous things all the time.

Dr. Carreon was a nice enough guy. He didn't have me lie down on a couch or anything. He just asked me to tell him about the situation, so I told him how much I loved jumping off things.

"Why do you think you need to play with danger like this, Johnny?" Dr. Carreon asked.

"I don't know," I replied. "It's fun, I guess."

"It's fun, yes. But perhaps there are other reasons. Things are not always what they seem on the surface. Sometimes people have very unusual reasons for doing the things they do."

"Like what?" I asked.

"For example, some kids in your school probably wear unusual clothing, or they get tattoos or pierce parts of their body. I suspect that many of these kids do that not because they like it, but because they hope to draw attention to themselves. It's an attention-getting device."

"I don't care if anybody's watching me."

"Then you obviously don't do it to get attention," Dr. Carreon said. "Maybe you simply have a Type T personality."

"What's that?"

"A Type T person is a natural risk taker. Some scientists believe risk taking is part of the American personality. People like George Washington, Lewis and Clark, and Amelia Earhart were probably Type Ts. They became national heroes because they took chances. But previous generations had to take risks every day. They had to worry about wild animals eating them. They had to worry about diseases like polio and influenza killing them. They had to worry about global wars. These days, life has become so comfortable that we don't face many challenges. Type T people want to find out what their limitations are. So they go in for extreme sports. They become gamblers. Or they risk their savings on the stock market. Or . . . maybe they become stuntmen."

"Hmmm," I replied, not knowing what else to say.

Dr. Carreon waited nearly a minute before posing the next question.

"Your father was a stuntman, correct?"

"Yes."

"And he died performing a stunt?"

"Yes."

"How did you feel about that, Johnny?"

"Bad."

"Can you elaborate?"

"He went over Niagara Falls in a boat that was supposed to turn into a plane. It never did."

"But how did it make you *feel*?" he pressed.

"Awful."

"Perhaps there is a genetic component," Dr. Carreon mused. "Your father may have passed on a thrill-seeking gene that controls the flow of certain chemicals in the brain."

"Maybe," I replied. So what if he did? I couldn't do anything about my genes.

"Or perhaps you're angry about your father's death and you channel that anger through self-destructive acts. On the other hand, you may be angry with *yourself*, believing you were somehow responsible for your father's accident. Maybe—just maybe—you have a death wish. Maybe your father did too. There could be any number of reasons why you do these things. I think we should explore this more tomorrow, Johnny."

What a crock, I thought when I left his office. I knew perfectly well why I liked doing dangerous things. It *felt* good!

When you're doing a stunt, time stands still for an instant. You don't think about your parents, your friends, your problems.

Nothing else matters. It just gives me some internal satisfaction and makes me feel alive. I like a challenge. I like to move fast. I like the feeling of wind rushing by me. I didn't need a psychologist to tell me that.

I gave the receptionist an envelope from Mom. I had checked, and there were five twenty-dollar bills inside. *A hundred bucks!* That was probably more money than Mom made all day. I vowed that I wouldn't go back to Dr. Carreon.

I don't steal. I don't smoke or drink or take drugs. But the next day I did a bad thing. I took the second $100 Mom gave me to pay Dr. Carreon and bought a pair of in-line skates with it.

Somebody had posted a notice on the bulletin board of the local supermarket. A guy was selling a brand-new pair of top-of-the-line, state-of-the-art skates worth $400. My size. Aluminum frame. Removable brake. Built-in shock absorbers. Eighty-millimeter wheels. Triple-density foam liner. The guy had broken his leg and wouldn't be needing the skates. He asked for $100, and I snapped them up.

After school the next day I was scheduled to see Dr. Carreon again. Instead, I went to this skate park in Venice, California, near where we live. It had lots of ramps, verts, half pipes, rails, and all kinds of cool stuff to jump over.

I had skated plenty of times before, but I never had a good pair of skates. I started doing some tricks, thinking the whole time that it was better therapy than talking with Dr. Carreon. I was eating the place up, really catching some big air, and noticed the other kids were watching me.

The next day I went to the skate park after school again. It wasn't very crowded yet so I pretty much had the place to myself. I had just ollied off the twelve-foot half pipe and went into an alley-oop hobo. That's when you spin 180 degrees and then jump on a rail backward. It's really hard to do, and you shouldn't even try it unless you're either really good or have a total lack of common sense.

I grinded down the rail, did a quick grab, bumped some stairs, and attempted a fishbrain. I didn't quite pull it off, and rag-dolled into the dirt.

When I looked up, there were two guys standing over me. One of them was a bald guy with a ponytail. That was the first time I met Roland Rivers.

"Rude, dude," Roland said in his British accent. "You must be a real hammerhead."

I'm always suspicious of grown-ups who try to talk the talk. "Thanks," was all I said, and started to skate away.

"May I rap with you for a moment, young man?" Roland asked.

"I don't talk to strangers," I replied.

"Smart boy," Roland said, handing me his business card. "Then allow me to introduce myself so we won't be strangers. My name is Roland Rivers, and I'm directing a film up the street. This is my assistant, Roger. Ever think of getting into movies?"

"Can't act," I said.

"Don't have to," Roland replied. "Can you do a back flip?"

I couldn't resist showing off a little. I skated over to an open area where there was a three-foot ramp and flipped head over heels. I'd done it plenty of times before. Then I skated back to him.

"Awesome!" he said, applauding. "You like things fast, don't you?"

"Yeah."

"Would you skate off the roof of a building?"

"Depends on the building."

"Out of a plane?"

"Maybe."

"Is it because you like excitement," Roland asked, "or are you just a fool?"

I looked at him. I wasn't sure if it was a serious question or a put-down.

"I like the excitement," I said, meeting his gaze.

"Did anybody ever tell you that you look a lot like Ricky Corvette?"

"Yeah, a few people."

Ricky Corvette hadn't made any movies at that point, but I had seen the TV show he was on. It was really awful, but a lot of seven-year-old kids thought it was cool. I *did* look a little like Ricky.

"Ricky has a part in a skating film I'm directing," Roland went on. "It's his first film. One scene calls for him to skate up a ramp and do a back flip."

"So?"

"I have just one problem—Ricky Corvette can't skate."

"So what's he doing in a skating movie?" I asked.

"America thinks he's cute."

"And you want me to skate in his place?"

"I already have a youngster skating for him," Roland said. "But the boy can't do a back flip. Maybe you could do it for him."

"Why should I?"

"I'll pay you $100."

"In real money?"

"Of course."

"Let's see it," I said. I still didn't trust Roland at that point.

Roland pulled out his wallet, peeled off a hundred-dollar bill, and handed it to me.

Back then, when I was ten, $100 was a lot of money to me. I'd never had a job. Never earned any money on my own. I'd never *seen* a hundred-dollar bill. I liked the look of it.

"What about your mom and dad?" Roland asked. "Are they going to be okay with this?"

"Don't have a dad," I said. "My mom won't care."

The second part was a lie, of course. But holding the bill in my hand made me feel better about buying the in-line skates with the $100 Mom had given me to pay Dr. Carreon.

I walked down the street with Roland to a big soundstage. I had never been on a movie set before, and it was pretty cool, seeing all those people and cameras and lights. Roland introduced me to Ricky Corvette, who I could tell right away was a jerk.

I did the back flip and was done in five minutes. Roland walked me out.

"There's more work like that if you want it," he said. "Why don't you come by tomorrow around the same time?"

"Okay."

"Hey, what's your name, son?"

"Johnny Thyme."

"Thyme?" Roland asked. "Are you any relation to Joe Thyme, the great stuntman?"

"He's . . . he was my dad."

"I'm sorry," Roland said. "It was terrible what happened at Niagara Falls. Your dad was perhaps the bravest stuntman who ever lived. He was an idol of mine. I always wished I'd get the chance to direct a film with him in it someday."

"Guess you'll have to settle for me instead."

"If you've got half the guts your father had, you'll go far."

I went back the next day and did a hand plant in front of

Roland's cameras. That's when you go upside down on a ramp in a handstand on a skateboard. It's also called an invert. Roland gave me another $100 and asked me to come back the following day. I did, and performed a 360 kick flip into a backside royale for him. Roland said there would be plenty more work like that, if I wanted it.

I could hardly believe it. Roland was paying me to do what I liked to do for the fun of it. I was having the time of my life.

At the end of that week, Mom called Dr. Carreon to ask him how I was doing in my therapy. He told her I hadn't shown up since the first appointment.

Mom was pretty PO'd, but I was ready for her. I gave her the $400 she had given me to pay Dr. Carreon, plus $400 more. I told her honestly how I'd earned the extra money.

"Instead of you paying all this money to a psychologist," I explained, "I'll give it back to *you*, and more. I promise I'll stop jumping off the garage and doing crazy stuff around the house, Mom. Please let me keep doing this. *Please*?"

Mom thought it over for a long time. When she let out a sigh, I knew I had won the argument.

And that's how I got my start doing stunts for Ricky Corvette.

9

WISHFUL THINKING

I was wrong about Boris Bonner. After I gave him the dollar bill on the first day of school, he didn't return it the next day. Or the day after that. When he came over to my locker after school a few days later, I had my hopes up that he was going to pay me. But all he did was stick out his hand—palm up. I could tell he didn't want me to slap him five.

"Hey Johnny Thyme," Boris said, "you got a dollar on you?"

"No."

It wasn't a lie. As it turned out, I *didn't* have a dollar on me. I had spent my extra money buying one of the pretzels the PTA ladies were selling in the cafeteria after lunch. But I was glad I didn't have a dollar, because I didn't want to give it to him.

"All I find I keep," Boris said.

He stuck his hands in the front pockets of my jeans. With his hands like that, it would have been so easy to punch him or slam my elbow against his head. It was tempting, but I didn't. I was scared. I didn't want to get into a fight and risk losing my job as Ricky Corvette's stuntman. Boris hadn't actually threatened me, but the threat was implied.

When he didn't find anything in my front pockets, Boris checked my back pockets. I could smell his cigarette breath as he reached around me.

"Lucky you weren't lying, Thyme," he said when my back pockets proved to be empty too. "It's not nice to lie."

"It's not nice to steal money either," I mumbled under my breath.

"What did you say?"

I looked around. The hallway was empty. Nobody was going to bail me out if I got into a fight.

"Nothing."

"Thyme," Bonner said, sticking his face next to mine, "I want you to do me a favor. I want you to bring me a dollar. On Monday. Bring it to school first thing in the morning. I'll meet you at the front of the school. Understand?"

"What for?" I asked.

"I'm low on cash."

"So am I."

"That's too bad, Thyme. Just bring me a dollar."

"And what if I don't?"

"If you don't," Bonner said, making a fist, "I'm gonna beat the crap out of you."

As Bonner walked away from me, I suddenly realized my heart was racing. I hadn't noticed it while he was shaking me down, but now that he was gone, my chest was pounding. I *never* should have given him that first dollar, I thought. It didn't get rid of him. It only showed him I was weak. Now I'd *never* get rid of him.

✖ ✖ ✖

As I walked home from school cursing myself for being so stupid, I couldn't help but think about Ricky Corvette. How come this sort of thing never happened to *him*, I wondered? Why is it that some kids lead a charmed life where everything always goes right?

I read Ricky's whole story in *People* magazine. When he was just a baby, his mother brought him to a modeling agency. He gurgled and cooed and laughed on cue. The camera loved him. By the time he was three, his picture had been on the package of every diaper, rattle, and stuffed animal in Toys "R" Us.

When he was five, Ricky beat out about a thousand other kids and landed the role of the adorable little boy with the cute voice on *Out of This World*. It was a dippy sitcom about a wacky family who move into the Mir space station after the astronauts move out. It was an instant hit, and suddenly everybody in America knew Ricky's name. The show ran for four years.

Apparently, Ricky's folks had trouble handling his success. His dad was a construction worker, and he didn't like the fact that his eight-year-old son made ten times more money than *he* did. He walked out on the family one day and didn't come back.

A year later, he had the nerve to sue Ricky and Ricky's mom. He claimed that he had supported the family during the years Ricky was growing up, so he was entitled to part of Ricky's future earnings—millions of dollars. The story was all over the tabloids. It was the first time a parent ever sued his own kid. Ricky's dad actually won the case, giving new meaning to the term *child support*.

Getting dragged through the courts made people feel sorry for Ricky. That made him more popular than ever and gave him more publicity. So he made *more* millions, and his dad wanted even *more* money. It was a real mess.

Come to think of it, Ricky Corvette's life wasn't so charmed after all.

Anyway, when *Out of This World* went off the air, Ricky made the jump to movies. He's a terrible actor, but he was in the right place at the right time, as usual. *Skate Fever* hit the theaters just as skateboarding and in-line skating were getting hot. All across America—and around the world—kids were trading in their balls, pucks, and racquets for Rollerblades, snowboards, mountain bikes, and other tools of the new "extreme sports."

Everybody in my school went to see *Skate Fever*, some of them over and over again. The movie made hundreds of millions of dollars. Ricky Corvette became a movie star. I was dying to tell everybody that it was *me* up there on the screen, not Ricky. But my contract, of course, prohibited telling anybody.

I did all of Ricky's stunts in *Skate Fever II*, *Skate Fever III*, and *Nightmare in L.A.* Roland directed them all. They were awful movies, but they were all hits. As Ricky became a Hollywood heavyweight, Roland was getting a reputation as the hot new director in town.

In those first few movies, Ricky had to do a lot of acting. But it didn't take long for the movie studio to figure out that audiences weren't coming to Ricky Corvette movies to see him act. They were coming to see Ricky jump off high objects, fly through the air, get himself into impossible predicaments and find a way out of them. All the stuff that I was actually doing in his place.

Every Ricky Corvette movie got more and more action oriented. By the time we made *New York Nightmare*, Ricky was hardly doing any acting at all.

So that's why I didn't spend my weekend worrying about Boris Bonner. I spent it risking my life at the top of the PsychoClone, the biggest and baddest roller coaster in the world.

We were filming a new action flick called *Great Adventure*. Here's the plot, if you can stomach it: The teenage daughter of the president of the United States invites her whole class to an amusement park for the day to celebrate the end of school. Some escaped prisoners who had been hiding out for a week in the haunted mansion find out the president's daughter is coming. They decide it would be the perfect opportunity to kidnap her. They do, threatening to kill her unless the president allows them to leave the country.

The girl finally gets rescued by a kid working in a cotton candy booth. He captures all the convicts and locks them up in the Ferris wheel cars until the police arrive to take them back to jail. The movie ends with the president pinning the Medal of Honor on the cotton candy vendor, who then plants a kiss on the "First Daughter."

Pretty sappy, huh?

The president's daughter was being played by the beautiful Augusta Wind. The cotton candy vendor was the one and only Ricky Corvette.

The climax of the film was the roller coaster scene. Roland and I worked all day on it. This was no run-of-the-mill dive-off-a-building gag. The script called for me to leap off a moving coaster.

It wouldn't be so tough on most roller coasters, but Psycho-Clone was no ordinary coaster. There was a sign at the bottom that said:

> PERSONS ARE NOT ALLOWED ON THIS RIDE IF
> THEY ARE PREGNANT, SUFFER FROM A HEART
> CONDITION, MOTION SICKNESS, BACK PROB-
> LEMS . . . OR HAVE A BRAIN IN THEIR HEAD.

Roland and I went over every inch of the track. The coaster starts with an eighty-foot lifthill, which immediately drops you into a 360-degree loop, followed by a boomerang, a corkscrew, and seven inversions. The top speed reaches seventy-two miles per hour at one point. At the top of one of the loops, there are three Gs pulling on your body.

If the riders haven't lost their lunch by that point, they still have to make it through six turning vertical dives, a 53-degree, 115-foot drop, and a two-story spiral. Then the whole sequence is repeated—backward!

It's tough enough to ride the PsychoClone when you're strapped into your seat, holding on for dear life. I would have to do it while a guy was trying to strangle me from behind with piano wire.

"It's going to be a piece of cake, Mr. Hangtime," Roland announced into his bullhorn. "I'll meet you at McDonald's."

I climbed down from the top and hopped into the first car. The actor playing the convict trying to kill me got into the seat behind me. He had a dummy next to him. A bunch of teenage extras—nonactors who fill out a crowd—climbed into the rest of the seats.

"Roll cameras!" bellowed Roland, and the coaster eased up the first incline. Roland had cameras positioned all over the track so he could shoot the action from many different angles.

We were halfway up the hill when the guy behind me—as instructed—slipped the wire over my head and around my neck. I reached up to protect my throat, and we struggled like that through the 360-degree loop.

While we were spinning through the boomerang, I managed to get the wire off my head. We wrestled with each other as the coaster shot through the corkscrew. In the middle of one of the inversions, I grabbed hold of the guy and threw him overboard to his death.

Actually, I grabbed hold of the *dummy* and threw *that* overboard, while the actor ducked below his seat. With all the screaming and the scenery flying by, the audience, hopefully, wouldn't notice.

My character appeared to think everything was fine, but during the vertical dive, *another* bad guy in the back car pulled out a gun and started shooting at me. Blanks, of course. I leaned forward and ducked my head. The bad guy fired off six shots. They ricocheted off the coaster. His seventh shot was a click. He was out of bullets.

The coaster slowly started climbing the last 115-foot lifthill. While leaning forward, I grabbed a prop umbrella, which had been placed at my feet. As the bad guy reloaded his gun, I popped open the umbrella and stepped up on my seat.

The coaster was at the crest of the hill now, about to shoot down the drop. Just as the bad guy was about to pull his trigger again, I jumped off the coaster, holding the umbrella. The coaster slid down the drop and I floated gently down.

It was difficult to control the umbrella, which had been specially designed to work like a parachute. When I hit the air bag placed on the ground alongside the ride, I twisted my right ankle and felt a sharp pain shoot up my leg. Right away I knew it was a bad sprain.

"Cut!" Roland screamed. "Awesome! Johnny, you are the man!"

As I hobbled off, I got a nice round of applause from the crew.

Meanwhile, Ricky Corvette was at home, probably lying around his pool and working on his tan. Roland would shoot some close-ups of his face later, but today Ricky wasn't even needed on the set.

Augusta Wind was, though. When we finished shooting the coaster scene, a limousine pulled up, and Augusta got out with her mother and her hair stylist. I was in a lot of pain, but like everyone else on the set I watched Augusta's every move. It was impossible to take your eyes off her.

Augusta didn't say a word to anybody, but her mom started jawing with Roland. She was upset because she had gone over the script and saw that Augusta only had a few lines to say in the whole movie. Roland promised to give her more, and that seemed to satisfy Augusta's mother.

Roland led Augusta to a coaster car that had been taken off the tracks and put on blocks. She stepped into it, followed by an actor holding a knife in his hand. A big fan was turned on to blow Augusta's hair around.

For the next half hour, Roland filmed Augusta screaming her head off while the guy held the knife to her throat. For somebody who hardly ever spoke, she sure could scream.

Finally, Roland yelled "Cut!" He would shoot the background scenes separately and put them together to make it look as though Augusta was on the coaster with the rest of us.

Her work done for the day, Augusta stepped out of the coaster and followed her mother into the waiting limousine. As usual, she didn't say a word to anybody.

My ankle was throbbing, and I should have left the set to care for it, but I couldn't stop staring at Augusta. What does a girl that beautiful think about, I wondered? Does she think at *all*? Can anyone that beautiful have any problems in her life?

I couldn't be sure, and maybe it was just wishful thinking, but as Augusta rolled up the window in her limousine, I thought for a moment that she might have smiled at me.

10

MIXED UP

Mom put ice on my ankle when we got home. That made the swelling go down, but she insisted on taking me to the doctor. He didn't put me in a cast or anything, but he had me fitted with a plastic brace to keep my ankle from moving. He gave me a pair of crutches and instructed me to use them for a week, even if the ankle felt fine.

When I got to school on Monday morning, Boris Bonner was waiting on the front steps. In all the excitement over the roller coaster stunt, I had forgotten that Bonner told me to bring in a dollar to school or he was going to beat me up.

Bonner took one look at me hobbling up the steps on crutches and broke into hysterical laughter. Some of the other kids turned to see what was so funny.

"Wimp!" he screamed gleefully. "Loser! Thyme, I can't believe you would lower yourself to faking an injury so I wouldn't beat you up!"

"I'm not faking an injury," I said, struggling up the steps. "I sprained my ankle."

"How?" Bonner asked gleefully. "You don't take gym. You don't play sports. You don't do *anything*!"

"I . . . tripped on my steps," I said.

"You are so pathetic, Thyme!" Bonner chortled. "You're not a man, you're a wimp."

As I hobbled past the line of laughing kids, for the first time in three years, I thought about giving up stunting. If I quit doing stunts, I would be like any other kid. I could take gym. I could go to dances. I could ride escalators. I could do anything I wanted. That included hauling off and socking a jerk like Boris Bonner if he gave me any trouble. And Mom would be thrilled if I quit.

For the time being, though, doing stunts was the one thing that allowed me to get *away* from my problems. The only time I could ever forget about people like Boris Bonner was when I was on a movie set, jumping off a building or doing some other crazy stunt.

I was all mixed up.

II

BLOWING /TUFF UP

"Let's blow something up today!" Roland exclaimed as he walked around the set, rubbing his hands together excitedly. "Anybody else in the mood to blow something up?"

Everybody agreed that blowing something up would be a terrific idea. The guys on movie crews always love blowing stuff up. This business must attract pyromaniacs. Personally, I think explosions are pretty cool, but I'd rather see them in the movies than in person.

My ankle had healed quickly. We were gathered at Buckeye Municipal Airport near Phoenix, Arizona. They had closed down part of the airport for the day so we could shoot this scene for *Great Adventure*. Roland had waited for a clear day with very little wind.

There were two planes on the ground, a new blue Cessna 150 and a red two-seater Jenny from the World War I era. The Jenny is a biplane, which means it has two sets of wings, one below the cockpit and the other above it. The cockpit is open to the wind.

Roland and the crew were going over camera angles, safety

precautions, and a million other details when Mom drove up in the old Ford Maverick she should have traded in years ago. Behind the Maverick was our horse trailer. As soon as I saw Squirt inside, I relaxed a little.

Squirt was a beautiful golden palomino that used to belong to my dad. I sort of grew up with him. When Dad died, Mom wanted to sell Squirt or give him away. It's expensive to feed and take care of a horse, and Mom told me we needed to save every penny we had.

I begged her not to get rid of Squirt, and she could see how much he meant to me. She agreed to let me keep him after one of the first stunts I did called for me to ride a horse. Squirt turned out to be a fine actor and stunt horse, so the studio paid Mom to use him in the film. He had been my stunt horse a number of times since then, so we could afford to keep him.

As she got out of the car, Mom had a worried expression on her face. It's the same expression she always has when I'm about to do a stunt. I said hi and backed Squirt out of the trailer. Roland came over to greet Mom with his usual enthusiasm.

"Meredith!" Roland bubbled. "How is it possible that you become more lovely with each passing day?"

"Roland, I need to talk to you," Mom said, ignoring his compliment and waving the script before him. "This scene makes no sense at all. The story is about the relationship between the president's daughter and this kid. The horse and plane stunt has nothing to do with anything. It doesn't move the story forward at all. It's totally superfluous."

"Superfluous" is one of Mom's favorite words. It means unnecessary. Mom reads all my scripts, and whenever she gets to one of my stunt scenes, she always says it's superfluous.

Roland took the script from Mom and looked it over for a few seconds. Then he pinched the pages between both hands, tore the script in half, and threw the pages up in the air. They scattered down the runway.

"Meredith," he said, wrapping an arm around Mom, "I'm perfectly aware that the horse and plane stunt doesn't move the story forward. I know that it's superfluous. And I don't give a flying fondue! The whole *movie* is superfluous!"

"So why do you have to shoot it?" Mom asked.

"Simple," Roland explained. "Moviegoers don't care about the relationship between two kids. They want to see somebody fall out of a plane and land on a horse. They want to see the plane explode in a huge fireball."

"That can't be true," Mom protested. "People have more brains than that."

"Sadly, it is true. You see, Meredith, people don't need to come to their local cineplex to see relationships. They can see relationships around their kitchen table every night. I want to give them something they *can't* see at home. Something they can't experience watching TV. Something they've never seen *anywhere*. I want to amaze people. I want to hear the audience say, 'How in the world did they *do* that?'"

"Then why don't you just make a movie with no dialogue at all?" Mom blustered. "Just wall-to-wall stunts from start to finish."

"That, Meredith, is my *dream*!" Roland's eyes were as big as golf balls. "All my life I have wanted to create a motion picture that has nothing but action from start to finish. No silly *dialogue* to get in the way and slow things down. Just continuous motion! That's why they call them *motion* pictures, don't you see? One of these days I'll make that film."

Mom saw that she was getting nowhere with Roland, so she turned to me.

"Johnny, please don't do it," she begged. "This gag is too dangerous."

"Mom, I've jumped out of plenty of planes."

"Not onto a horse!"

"It's perfectly safe, Mom. Roland wouldn't let me do it if it wasn't safe."

"Meredith," Roland interrupted, "I understand your concern. But I assure you, Johnny will be safer than he is when you tuck him into bed at night. May I suggest you and I discuss this over dinner this evening? I know this charming little bistro—"

"Sure," Mom agreed, making Roland's eyes light up. "I'll have dinner with you tonight—if you cut the scene, Roland."

"Oh, Meredith, why must you torture me so?"

Roland paced up and down the runway for a few minutes, his hands clasped behind his back. Everybody stood around waiting for him. Finally he came back and clapped his hands together.

"Okay, everybody, let's blow something up!"

Mom marched away angrily.

I adjusted my goggles and parachute and climbed aboard the red Jenny. The pilot, Sam Solomon, was also a stuntman. He climbed into the seat in front of mine.

Roland did a final check to see if the cameras mounted on the Cessna were working properly. When he was satisfied, he climbed in behind the pilot. The two planes taxied down the runway together.

"Meet you at Burger King!" I yelled to Roland.

As we took off I leaned out and waved to Mom. Sam brought our Jenny up to five thousand feet and leveled off at that altitude. The Cessna pulled alongside ours and got as close as it could without touching wings. Roland gave us the okay sign, which meant we could start the scene whenever we were ready.

Sam put the Jenny on autopilot and climbed out of his seat onto the left wing. Carefully, *very* carefully, I followed.

Sitting inside the enclosed cabin of a jet plane doesn't really give you the true experience of flying. I say if you really want to fly, you have to stand out on the plane's wing while the plane is in midair, going a hundred miles an hour or more. *Feel* the wind shoot by you. *Hear* the roar of the engine. *Feel* the cold moisture of a cloud as it hits you in the face. *Realize* that if you slip, your life is over.

Now *that's* flying!

"Wing walking" is a movie tradition that goes back to the barnstorming pilots of the 1920s. The old biplanes are still used for these scenes because the struts and wires that connect the two wings give wing walkers lots of places to grab hold.

The cockpit of our Jenny had been moved back a few feet to compensate for the added weight Sam and I would be putting on the front of the plane. A 600-horsepower engine had been installed too, because it needed extra power.

The script called for Sam and me to fight with each other out on the wing. I had done fight scenes before, but always on the ground. In this scene, whoever lost the fight would get knocked out—out of the plane, that is.

Still, a fight is a fight. Sam and I had practiced on the ground with Roland until we knew the fight scene by heart. Each of us would be throwing five carefully choreographed punches. According to the script, my fifth punch would knock Sam off the wing.

Movie fights are nothing like real fights. You've got to telegraph your punches so the guy you're about to punch can see it coming. Actors are trained to throw long, looping punches with the widest possible arc. If you throw a punch like that in a *real* fight, you'll get clobbered. That's why good boxers make terrible movie fighters.

Sam and I couldn't talk to each other. The noise of the engine and air whipping by us was too loud. We faced off against each other on the left wing. Being careful to keep my fist loose so it wouldn't hit with too much force, I punched Sam in the stomach. Immediately I got into position for Sam's return blow.

Sam doubled over, then straightened up and socked me with an uppercut to the jaw. It just missed me, but I fell backwards to make it look real, grabbing a strut as my back hit the wing.

I struggled to get up and Sam tried to kick me, but I grabbed his leg and pulled it, causing him to fall down too. As he held on to the wires with each hand, I leaped on top of him and punched him in the face with my left, then right, then left hand again. We rolled over and Sam did the same to me. My head was hanging over the wing and Sam put both hands around my neck, pretending to choke me.

As this was happening, I sneaked a peek at Roland in the Cessna. He was loving it.

I managed to get Sam's hands off me, and each of us threw another punch. After I threw mine, Sam went flying off the wing backward. He had to be careful not to get hit by the tail of the plane, or he would be knocked unconscious. Not a good idea when you're five thousand feet up.

Once he was out of camera range, Sam opened up the parachute that was hidden underneath his jacket. In the movie, it would look like he had fallen off the plane to his death.

The script called for my character to do a triumphant "end zone dance" on the wing, and then suddenly realize the pilot is gone and he doesn't know how to fly the plane. I did that, then rushed to the cockpit. As instructed, I flipped a switch on the dashboard to turn off the engine. It sputtered and the propeller stopped. This plane was going down.

Quickly I reached under the pilot's seat, where a snowboard was hidden. I raced back out on the wing with it and attached the snowboard to my feet. When I was sure it was secure, I took a deep breath and jumped off the wing.

I know what you're thinking. Why was there a snowboard hidden in the plane? Why did my character put it on his feet? Why didn't he just try to land the plane instead?

The answer to these questions is simple: How should I know? Roland said it would look cool.

"Everybody has seen planes land," he explained as we were going over the gag. "But how many people have seen a kid snowboard out of a plane?"

He was right, of course. I had done quite a bit of skydiving, but the snowboard made it more interesting. It slowed my descent, and the extra air resistance enabled me to do some cool tricks. By tilting my feet, I could make my body move left, right, and even flip around head over heels. It was awesome. I just hoped Roland's cameras were getting it all on film.

I was having such a good time that I nearly forgot to open my parachute. This can be dangerous, as you might imagine.

In any fall, you have to first know your altitude at the top, then calculate how many seconds until you would hit the ground, how long it will take your parachute to open fully, and how long you can wait before opening the parachute. Roland worked this all out ahead of time, so I knew to count to eight before pulling my ripcord.

I opened the chute and it yanked me hard when the cloth filled with air. It feels like you're moving upward at that moment, but actually you're not. It's just that you're decelerating—slowing down—so quickly.

As soon as I opened my chute, Roland's Cessna headed down. Below me, I saw the red Jenny plummet earthward. It got smaller and smaller until it exploded in a fireball below.

As I floated down, I kicked the snowboard off my feet and looked around, searching for Squirt. After a few anxious seconds, I spotted him galloping a few hundred yards away.

I didn't want Squirt to see me in front of him because he might get spooked and change direction. I maneuvered my chute around so that I would come down behind him.

Roland had said that this gag would be a movie first. Nobody had ever fallen out of the sky and landed on a horse before. It was not the kind of gag I could rehearse over and over again. I had to get it right the first time.

A few hundred feet over Squirt, I estimated that I was a little higher than I wanted to be. If I kept going like that, I would touch down in front of Squirt and he might trip over me. I pulled the cord that gives the chute a little less forward lift. It worked. I came down smoothly and only had to make a few minor left and right adjustments.

I landed on Squirt's back with a gentle thud. Squirt didn't miss a stride. The parachute collapsed to the ground behind me.

"Good boy!" I yelled in Squirt's ear. I gave him a pat on the side of his head and pulled a carrot out of my pocket for him.

It took a few minutes for Roland's plane to land, and a few more for him to hop in a jeep and meet me.

"Awesome!" Roland shouted when he caught up with me. His face was flushed red. "Absolutely awesome!"

12

THE ULTIMATE

After I finished doing the stunts for *Great Adventure*, I didn't hang around to watch Ricky Corvette and Augusta Wind shoot their usual lovey-dovey scenes. I was anxious to get back home, back to my old bed. Sleeping in hotels and motels gets old after a while. Mom and I packed up Squirt in the trailer and pointed the old Maverick toward California.

It was December, and I was looking forward to Christmas vacation. I wouldn't have to deal with Boris Bonner—or anything else—for three whole weeks. Walking home from school that day, I was feeling pretty good.

"Hey, Thyme!"

I turned around. It was Bonner. Nobody was around to bail me out, as usual.

"Gimme a dollar, Thyme."

I stopped and faced him.

"No," I said.

"All I find I keep, Thyme."

I was sick of Bonner. I didn't care about the rules anymore. I didn't care about my contract. I didn't care about doing stunts. As Bonner slid his hands into my front pockets, I reached my elbow back and slammed it against the side of his head with all the force I could generate.

I don't think anything ever felt so good in my whole life.

It took him completely by surprise, knocking Bonner sideways and off his feet. He lay on the ground and rubbed his jaw for a moment before looking up at me.

"Big mistake," Bonner said, getting to his feet slowly. "I might not see you over the holidays, so I'm going to have to give you a beating that will last you until New Year's."

Bonner advanced on me, churning his fist in front of him like a bag full of rocks. There was some blood on his right cheek.

I backed up a few steps so I would be able to plant my foot and get a good shot at him. Bonner must not have been much of a boxer, because instead of hitting me, he grabbed me in a bear hug and wrestled me on the ground.

We rolled around like that, trying to punch and choke each other. I got in a few shots, and so did he.

Suddenly, a car screeched to a halt next to us. I didn't stop. I didn't care. I wanted to do as much damage to Bonner as I could before anybody stopped the fight.

"Break it up, boys!" a familiar voice shouted, "Knock it off!"

Hopping out of the car was Roland Rivers.

He was much bigger and stronger than both Bonner and me, so he was able to separate us by force.

"You're dead, Thyme!" Bonner shouted, as Roland pulled us apart. "Dead!"

I replied by saying some words I'm not ever supposed to say, but words you've probably heard around the schoolyard. I think you know what I mean.

Neither of us won the fight. I'd call it a tie. But Bonner strode away, swinging his shoulders as though he had whipped me good. I couldn't help but laugh.

"Are you crazy, Johnny?" Roland asked as he straightened out my shirt. "If word about this ever got back to Ricky Corvette's people, you'd never work in movies again! Your contract strictly forbids fight—"

"I quit, Roland," I interrupted. "I don't want to work in movies anymore. I've had it."

Roland's face turned pale. He leaned against his car heavily, like *he* had just been in a fight.

"It's no big deal," I told him, "You can get somebody else to do stunts for Ricky Corvette. Plenty of kids can do what I do."

"No," Roland insisted. "Somebody as good as you comes along only once every generation. First came your dad, then you. No other kid can do what I have in mind."

"What do you mean, have in mind?"

"That's what I came to talk to you about," Roland explained. "Remember I told you about my dream of making a film with just stunts from start to finish?"

"Yeah."

"Well, it's going to come true."

Roland told me that the last few Ricky Corvette/Augusta Wind films had been huge hits for Spectra Films, the small company that gave Ricky his start. Now, Paramount—a major motion picture company—had decided to do a big-budget movie starring Ricky and Augusta. They wanted Roland to write and direct it, and he had complete creative freedom. Paramount was giving him $200 million to play with. That's much more than Roland usually gets.

"Two hundred million, Johnny!" he exclaimed. "Do you know how much stuff we can blow up with two hundred million dollars?"

"I can imagine," I replied.

"I wrote this script," he said, reaching into his car. "Ricky plays this secret agent, sort of a teenage James Bond. You get to ski off a mountain, Johnny! There will be some underwater work. Car crashes. Lots of high falls. A chase scene on Jet Skis."

It sounded like it would be a blast to shoot.

"A horse scene, a fire scene, some fistfights," Roland continued. "The story makes no sense at all, Johnny, but it's great! I'm going to shoot it on location, so you'll get to travel all over the world. This will be the ultimate action movie, Johnny! Wall-to-wall stunts! This is the film I've dreamed about all my life!"

The intensity in his eyes told me he meant every word he was saying. I knew that if I turned him down, Roland would be crushed.

"What's it called?" I asked.

"*Two Birds, One Stone.* See, this madman has to kill Ricky and Augusta together so he can take over the world. And here's the best part. Guess how many lines of dialogue Ricky will have?"

"I give up."

"Seven!" Roland exclaimed gleefully.

"That's *all*?"

"That's all! Paramount knows Ricky can't act for beans. They said it's fine with them if I just use him for the close-ups. The rest of the movie is just you. This is *your* movie, Johnny! I'm telling you, it will be endorphin city! I was hoping to start shooting during your winter vacation. Are you with me?"

Roland looked at me with those big puppy-dog eyes of his. He looked like he was about to cry. One more movie couldn't hurt, I guessed.

"Okay, I'll do it," I said, and Roland wrapped his big arms around me in a bone-crunching bear hug.

"There's one thing you should know, Johnny." Roland suddenly sounded serious.

"What is it?"

"There's a Niagara Falls scene."

That froze me. I hadn't thought about Niagara Falls in a long time. I hadn't been back to the Falls since my dad died. It had been three years.

There was no cemetery I could visit. No tombstone I could stand in front of and imagine my father lying beneath. Going back to Niagara Falls would be the closest thing to visiting my father's grave. It would be a way to honor his memory.

"It's an awesome scene, Johnny," Roland said, "but I'll cut it if you want me to."

"Don't cut it, Roland."

"Johnny, you don't have to do it."

"I *want* to do it."

"Are you sure?"

"I'm sure."

"You'd better talk it over with your mother first," he said, handing me the script. "She might not feel the same way you do."

I didn't tell Mom about the fight with Bonner or about Roland's visit. I wanted to look over the script for *Two Birds, One Stone* first.

Roland wasn't exaggerating. There was hardly any story to the movie at all. It was just one action scene after another. It looked great.

The Niagara Falls gag would have me in a canoe going down the Niagara River. Just as the canoe is about to go over the Falls, a rescue helicopter would swoop down and carry me to safety. It was the last scene in the script. It would be dangerous, of course. But not as dangerous as going down the river in a boat that was supposed to sprout wings.

When Mom came home from work that day, I didn't tell her about the script. There was no way she was going to let me do a Niagara Falls gag. Not after what happened to Dad.

There wasn't much to say over dinner. All I could think about was *Two Birds, One Stone*.

I had a few options before me. I could be honest with Mom. I could tell her what Roland told me, show her the script, and plead my case. If she said doing the movie was out of the question, I could simply defy her, claiming I'm old enough to make my own decisions. Or, I could make Mom happy and quit doing stunts for good. Mom would probably be so thrilled, she'd go out to dinner with Roland.

Then another option occurred to me. Examining the script, I saw that the final scene of *Two Birds, One Stone*—the Niagara Falls scene—filled pages 115 and 116 completely. The previous action scene ended on page 114.

I took pages 115 and 116 and threw them in the trash.

Then I went out to the garage and got Mom's old typewriter. I rolled page 114 into the typewriter until it was at the bottom of the page. There, I typed the words THE END.

Anybody reading the script would get to the bottom of page 114 and think the movie was over. There was no way to tell an entire scene had been cut out.

I felt bad about what I did, but I didn't know what else to do. I really wanted to do the movie, and I knew Mom would never let me.

I knew I'd have to tell her eventually, but I figured I would cross that bridge when I came to it.

The next night, when Mom came home, I told her about *Two Birds, One Stone* and gave her the script. As she read it, I pretended to be watching TV but actually watched her out the corner of my eye. I tried not to let on that I was nervous. I hoped she wouldn't notice that the typewriting at the bottom of page 114 didn't exactly match the rest of the script.

"Superfluous . . . superfluous . . . superfluous," was all she said as she flipped the pages.

Finally, Mom reached the last page. She sighed, closed the script, and looked at me.

"I don't like it," she said, making my heart sink. "It's the same old junk, just more of it. But I don't see anything in here that's worse than the other gags you've done."

"So I can do it?"

"If you want to."

"You're the best mom in the whole world!"

13

TWO BIRDS, ONE STONE

A week later, I still hadn't figured out a way to break the news about the Niagara Falls scene to Mom. We hadn't shot one second of film yet, but reports about *Two Birds, One Stone* were already turning up in magazines and on TV.

People were saying this would be the movie where Ricky Corvette would grow up. He would stop playing a cute kid and take on his first role as a young man. Very few child stars grow up to become adult movie stars. Everybody wanted to know if Ricky could make that leap. If he flopped, his career would probably be over.

The cast and crew of *Two Birds, One Stone* gathered at Paramount Pictures in Hollywood. Mom drove me over to the enormous sound-stage, and Roland gathered everybody around him to talk us through the movie.

"Ladies, gentlemen," Roland said, pacing back and forth. "We're going to make movie history. *Two Birds, One Stone* is going to be bigger than *Star Wars*. Bigger than *Titanic*. It will have more action, more stunts, more excitement than any film that came before it. The audience will leave the theater shaking their heads in astonishment."

Roland glanced at me and Mom before continuing. "But the most important thing is not how exciting it will be or how much money this movie is going to make. The most important thing is that nobody gets hurt."

Satisfied that I wouldn't get killed—at least not *that* day—Mom gave me a hug and left so she could get to work on time.

The only two people who missed the meeting were Ricky and Augusta. They were shooting a Pepsi commercial together in Tahiti, and would join the rest of us in a few weeks. In the meantime, Roland explained, we had to begin shooting the action scenes.

It would be fairly easy to shoot around Ricky and Augusta, because the movie was almost all action. Roland told us he would shoot the simplest stunts first, saving the big one for the end. That way, I supposed, if I got killed going over Niagara Falls, at least the film would be finished.

Paramount's lawyers arrived on the set, and Roland warned us they would be keeping an eye on things. We broke up the meeting and the crew set up for the first gag.

Picture this: I am sitting atop Squirt, who seems to have a bit of the sniffles today. The script calls for a team of bad guys with guns to be chasing me down a city street. I leap on a policeman's horse—Squirt—and the bad guys start shooting at me. They hit Squirt instead of me, and he falls down while I escape.

They're not going to actually shoot Squirt, of course. He's got to fall down on his own. Back in the old days, when they needed a horse to fall in a movie, they used what was called a running W—two criscrossed trip wires. The rider would yank them at the proper moment, and the horse's feet would be pulled out from under him.

Animal rights groups put a lot of pressure on the movie industry to ban the running W, because many of the horses were getting hurt. These days, they train horses to fall on command. Squirt has fallen hundreds of times. My dad taught him how to do it when Squirt was very young.

"Roll camera!" Roland shouted. "Meet you at Taco Bell!"

I snapped the reins once and Squirt galloped off. Carefully, I eased my left foot into the step stirrup. That's a little step that is placed on the side of the saddle away from the camera. As we approached the camera, I shifted my weight to that side.

"Down Squirt, down!" I hollered, pulling on the reins.

Squirt let his front legs collapse and rolled his body left. Before he hit the dirt, I jumped off the step stirrup and fell clear of him. I landed on the bed of cork and soft dirt that had been prepared for me, tumbling over a few times so there was no chance Squirt would hit me. It was a perfect fall, I thought.

"Cut!" Roland yelled. "Let's try that one more time, Johnny."

Roland explained to me that the fall looked a bit fake to him. I had jumped off too soon, before Squirt reacted to being shot. Roland was right, as usual. I had to be careful not to anticipate so much.

We shot the scene again and then a third time because Roland wasn't happy with the lighting. Finally he got what he was looking for, and the crew gave Squirt and I a nice round of applause.

"Good boy," I whispered into Squirt's ear. He got up gingerly and I led him to the trailer for Mom to take him home later.

Next scene. Picture this: I am in the Trikes & Bikes store at the Anaheim mall. The entire mall has been closed for the day so we can shoot the movie here.

It's a complicated gag. The script calls for Ricky to be testing this hot new mountain bike as if he is thinking of buying it; however, some bad guys get there first and plant a bomb to kill him. It explodes in a ball of fire, blowing him ten feet, through the front window of the store, and into the fountain in the middle of the mall. Roland wants to get it all in one take.

"Roll cameras!" he booms.

"Meet you at KFC!" I yell back.

I am wearing three layers of fire resistent underwear. On top of that and under my clothes is a Kevlar fireproof suit. I'm already sweating because my skin can't breathe. But then again, I don't want it to.

My face is covered by a nonflammable silicone mask that looks vaguely like Ricky Corvette's face. My hands have to be covered with flesh-colored silicone too. It would look dumb if I were wearing fireproof gloves inside.

An ice cold, gooey gel made from a rare tropical plant has been smeared all over me. It doesn't stop the burning, but it increases your body's tolerance to heat. On top of that is a layer of flammable glue.

Even with all this on your body, a stuntman can't do a full fire burn longer than a minute or two. I've come pretty close a few times, and it's not fun. First, you start feeling warm. Then you feel hot. After that . . . well, you *bake* to death. I'm just thankful Mom couldn't make it to see this. She told me she had to stay home because the vet was coming over to take a look at Squirt.

Behind me, the pyro guys have rigged up a fake bomb composed of flash powder, rubber cement, and this black powder called naphthalene that smells like mothballs. You light up a few hundred pounds of that stuff and it makes a fireball that'll burn your eyelids off if you're not careful.

I take a deep breath from the air tube one of the grips holds up to my mouth. She takes the tube away and I close my mouth tightly.

"Three . . . two . . . one . . . "

The blast goes off. As soon as the fire licks the flammable glue, I am engulfed in flames. My body is a human torch. Thanks to all the fire protection, I don't feel a thing.

The explosion was designed to *look* powerful, but it really isn't. To launch me and the bike, Roland installed an air ram in the floor under me. It's a pneumatic device that pushes up with 2,000 pounds of pressure per square inch to shoot you into the air.

The air ram fires and I feel like I've left my stomach behind. I am on the bike, in a full burn, flying straight toward the front window of the store. I have no control. It's a no-brainer. That's what stunt guys call a gag in which you're just a passenger.

A body that shattered real glass would be sliced into a million pieces, of course. In the early days of the movies, they used candy glass for window-breaking scenes. It was this sugar-based stuff that was rolled to the thickness of a window—sort of like a lollipop window.

The problem was that candy glass melted under hot lights. Nowadays they have thin plastics that look and shatter just like real glass. I must have flown through a hundred windows over the last three years. It's fun!

The front wheel of the bike crashes through the window, and pieces of "glass" are flying all around me. I don't feel it, just as I don't feel the flames that are burning away my clothes.

The next part of the gag is actually the most dangerous—landing in the fountain. Roland didn't want me to land *with* the bike because it could slip on the water and break a lot of bones (mine). His first thought was to have me wear a jerk vest attached to a thin wire that would pull me off the bike after I crashed through the window. But he was afraid the flames might burn through the vest. Instead, he decided to attach a wire to the *bike*, and yank it out from under me before I hit the fountain.

I am about ten feet from the fountain. I feel the pull on the bike. I let go of the handlebars and the bike flies out of harm's way. The fountain is coming up fast. If I land in the water, it will put the flames out immediately. If I miss, crash pads surround the fountain. A bunch of guys with wet blankets and fire extinguishers are also stationed around to smother the flames if they have to.

The water is only two feet deep. I spread out my arms and legs to distribute the impact of the water across my whole body. I struggle to keep my head up. The one part of your body you don't want to slam into anything is your head. It's not like you can put a cast on it and it will heal in six weeks.

You would think water would be a soft place to land, but in fact, it feels like concrete. I prepare for the impact and belly flop into the middle of the fountain. The flames are extinguished immediately. Water sloshes all over the place. I gasp for air. As I open my eyes and rip the mask off my face, everybody on the crew is cheering.

"Cut!" Roland shouts. "Superb!"

The whole sequence—from explosion to splashdown—has taken less than two seconds. In slo-mo, it will take up about ten seconds of screen time. And, from preparation to cleanup, the scene has taken all day to shoot.

You think *you* had a tough week? On Tuesday, I got into an underwater fight with a lunatic wielding a harpoon. On Wednesday, I got thrown out of a car's sunroof and had to ski off a mountain. On Thursday, I had to jump off a train onto a Jet Ski. On Friday, I had to cross a broken rope bridge while some guys were setting it on fire.

But Saturday was the worst day of the week—Mom showed up.

Not that I wasn't happy to see her. But as soon as I saw her, I could tell something was wrong. She has a very easily readable face.

Mom hadn't been able to spend much time on the set with me. She had used up all her vacation days at work and her boss was starting to give her a hard time about taking days off.

"Johnny," she said as soon as she stepped out of the car, "I have bad news. I had to have Squirt put to sleep."

I didn't cry. Actors know how to cry. Stuntmen know how *not* to. I cried on the inside. Squirt had been more than a pet to me. We worked together. He saved my butt a few times. And he was a living reminder of my dad.

Mom told me that when we shot the routine horse fall, Squirt had hurt his left front leg pretty badly. Because horses weigh close to two thousand pounds, it's very difficult for their damaged legs to heal properly. Even if a cast is put on it, the horse can't be ridden again.

The vet made it as painless as possible, Mom assured me. Squirt was sedated first, then given a lethal injection of phenobarbitol.

Roland came over to flirt with Mom, but he saw right away that something was wrong.

"Squirt's dead," I said, and I told him what happened.

Roland started sobbing quietly, and then the dam burst open. Big tears slid down his cheeks. He didn't bother wiping them away, and they gathered in his beard. Then he began bawling loud enough for both of us. I'd never seen a man break down the way he did.

I guess Roland felt somewhat responsible. If he hadn't shot the horse fall scene three times, maybe Squirt wouldn't have hurt himself.

"Meredith," Roland apologized through his tears. "I'm so sorry. If I was in any way responsible—"

"You weren't, Roland," Mom assured him. "Squirt was old. The vet said it was only a matter of time."

"I assure you, this is the safest set I've ever worked on. You will not regret allowing Johnny to do this film. It showed tremendous courage and faith on your part, especially in light of what happened to your husband. When we shoot the Niagara Falls gag, every safety precaution will be in place."

Uh-oh.

"What Niagara Falls gag?" Mom asked.

I tried to slink away, but Mom grabbed me by the collar.

"Didn't you read Johnny's script, Meredith?" Roland asked.

"Of *course* I read Johnny's script!"

Roland handed her his copy of the script and opened it up to the last two pages—the pages I had removed from the copy I showed to Mom. She read it, then turned to me. I thought fire was going to come out of her eyes.

"You tricked me!" she barked.

"I didn't know what to do!" I whined. "I knew you'd never let me do the movie, and I wanted to do it so badly."

"You're *just* like your father!"

I always suspected she was afraid I would turn out like my dad, but that was the first time she ever came out and said it. Maybe she was right. Maybe I *was* just like my dad.

"That's it," Mom said, grabbing my hand. "Johnny, we're going home."

"But Mom!"

"We can't stop the film now!" Roland exclaimed. "Paramount has already invested a hundred fifty million in it."

The mention of money made the Paramount lawyers flit over like moths to a flame. They said all kinds of things that made no sense to me: "commitment" . . . "breach of contract" . . "escape clause." I didn't understand all the terms, but I got the idea. The long and short of it was, if Mom pulled me out of the movie, Paramount would take legal action against her.

"I'm sorry," I kept telling her, but it didn't do any good.

Mom was furious, but she realized there was nothing she could do about it. She doesn't know any high-powered lawyers.

"If anything happens to Johnny," she warned Roland, "it will be *your* fault."

No matter what, I would have to make the Niagara Falls gag work.

LIAR

By the second week of January we had finished all the stunt work for *Two Birds, One Stone* except for the Niagara Falls scene. Everything had gone smoothly. I hadn't suffered so much as a mosquito bite, and Mom was starting to relax a little bit. The speaking parts hadn't been shot yet because Ricky and Augusta weren't back from Tahiti. They were scheduled to meet us at Niagara Falls, where we'd finish up the film.

The TV was on as Mom and I were packing for the trip to Niagara Falls. I wasn't really paying attention, but the words "Ricky Corvette" found my ears and I looked up. *Entertainment Tonight* was on and Ricky's obnoxious face filled the screen. Mom knows how much I hate Ricky, and she grabbed for the remote to change the channel. But I got to it first.

> Host: "Ricky, what's happening with you and Augusta Wind? Are you going steady? Might there be marriage in your future?"
>
> Ricky: "We're only fifteen! Augusta and I are just good friends. She's a terrific girl."
>
> Host: "Is it true that you and Augusta are working on a new film together?"
>
> Ricky: "Yes, Two Birds, One Stone. It's going to be a real edge-of-your-seat, hide-your-eyes, I-can't-believe-he's-doing-that kind of action movie from start to finish. This time, man, I'm gonna get the law of gravity repealed. I hope everyone will go see it."
>
> Host: "Ricky, with every movie you do, more and more action seems to get packed into your scenes. There have been rumors that you rely heavily on professional stunt-men. Any truth to that?"
>
> Ricky: "That's ridiculous! I do all my own stunts. Always have. Doing my own stunts is how I express myself as an artist. I look at it this way: If you're not living on the edge, man, you're taking up too much room."

"Liar!" I screamed, throwing a sneaker at the TV screen. "How can he say that with a straight face?"

"What do you expect him to say?" Mom said calmly, changing the channel before I could hear the rest of the interview. "He's an actor, and he's got his image to protect. You know what you've accomplished. That's all that matters."

I felt like my blood was boiling. It never really bothered me that I didn't get the credit for what I did in Ricky Corvette's movies. But we were nearly finished with *Two Birds, One Stone* and I had done *everything*. Ricky wasn't even on the screen yet. When he flat-out lied on national television, it pushed some kind of button in me and made me furious.

As Mom and I flew to Niagara Falls the next day, I stewed the whole way.

15

CONFRONTATION

Mom and I checked into the Sheraton Fallsview Hotel, which overlooks Niagara Falls. I could hear the roar of the water from our room. When I went to the window, I could see the falls.

It had been three years since the accident, but I had a mental videotape of the stunt that would stay with me forever. Dad was wearing a tuxedo, confidently piloting the boat down the river. He had shown me the boat earlier in the day, when it was still on land.

"Stand clear!" he'd said. Then he pushed a button on the dashboard and the two wings popped out of the side of the boat. "Is that cool or what?"

He tested it ten or fifteen times, and there was never any problem. But then, the only time it mattered, the wings didn't pop out.

The boat had been equipped with a parachute in case of emergency. I saw it come out. But it must have become tangled up or caught by the spray of water, because it never fully opened. The boat just dropped like a brick. It must have been awful. But knowing my dad, if he had been given a choice of dying peacefully in his sleep or going over Niagara Falls, he probably would have picked the falls.

Mom closed the shades and turned on the TV to drown out the sound of the water.

The schedule that Roland handed out called for us to spend three days at Niagara Falls. On Saturday, he would shoot some background scenes and the crew would prepare for what he called the big gag—the helicopter rescue. On Sunday we'd shoot the big gag. On Monday, Ricky and Augusta would do their talking scenes.

Early on Saturday morning, the lighting guys, prop guys, grips, gaffers, and gofers gathered around Roland in the hotel parking lot, where they had set up a little tent city. There was a food truck for when we had the munchies, and portable toilets for when we had to go. Everybody was busy, going about their business getting ready to finish up the movie. There must have been a few hundred people scurrying around.

All activity stopped when a white, impossibly long limousine pulled up. Ricky Corvette and Augusta Wind stepped out, followed closely by their mothers. Ricky shook hands with Roland and greeted a few of the cameramen he knew. Augusta—looking more spectacular than ever—didn't say a word to anybody.

Within seconds a buzz had traveled through the crowd, like a wave at a ballgame.

"Ricky's voice changed!"

"Ricky's voice changed!"

"Ricky's voice changed!"

Watching Ricky Corvette was like watching a horror movie. I didn't want to look, but I had to look anyway. I pushed up closer. I hadn't seen Ricky in a few months.

At first, I almost didn't recognize him. He looked older. He wasn't as cute as he used to be. Ricky still had that good-looking baby face, but there was a sprinkling of zits on it. Too many M&Ms, I guessed. Puberty can really do a number on a guy, and fast.

Makeup could hide the zits, but it couldn't do much for his body. His arms and legs didn't quite fit anymore. He looked gawky, awkward. Ricky had put on some weight too. If he resembled a young Elvis before, now he looked like the *old* Elvis. The fat, sweaty, Vegas Elvis.

Ricky was smoking a cigarette, undoubtedly because he thought it made him look older, or cooler, or maybe he was just trying to kill himself as slowly as possible.

Then there was that *voice*. Ricky always had this adorable little boy voice. It was a big part of his appeal. When I was about ten feet away from him, I could tell it was gone. His voice was lower and deeper than before, but not quite as low and deep as a man's voice. It was somewhere in the middle. His voice cracked, like a door that needs to be oiled.

His voice may have changed, but Ricky was just as much of a jerk as ever. He didn't say hello to me. He didn't ask how I was, or how the movie had been going.

"Hey, stuntkid," he said when he saw me. "Get me a Mountain Dew."

I had always tried to be as nice as possible to Ricky, no matter how awful he acted. But after seeing him on *Entertainment Tonight*, I wasn't in the mood to do him any favors.

"I hear you do all your own stunts," I replied. "So you can get your *own* Mountain Dew."

Ricky looked at me with his eyes wide open, like he couldn't believe anyone would dare to address him in such a disrespectful manner.

"If it weren't for me," he growled, "you'd be flipping burgers at McDonald's."

"If it weren't for *me*," I shot back, "you'd be sweeping the *floor* at McDonald's. I doubt you have the hand-eye coordination to flip burgers."

I thought Ricky was going to slug me, which would have been great. I knew I could flatten that weasel with one punch. I was ready for him. But he just stormed away and found somebody else to get him a Mountain Dew.

Word quickly swept around the set that I had stood up to the great Ricky Corvette. I was getting high fives and thumbs-up signs for the rest of the day.

It was probably a mistake to get into a war with a Hollywood heavyweight like Ricky. But I didn't care. I had other things to worry about. Tomorrow, I would be going to the brink of Niagara Falls in a canoe.

16

THE COWARD

The clock said it was 1:30 A.M., but I wasn't tired. The constant rumble of Niagara Falls was pounding against my ears. I looked over at the bed next to mine and saw that Mom was asleep.

There was nothing to worry about, really. Roland and I had gone over the gag repeatedly. I would paddle the canoe out to the middle of the river a few miles upstream from the falls. The river moves fast, up to forty miles per hour in some places.

A helicopter would be right above me, but out of camera range. When I reached the edge of the falls, it would swoop down. All I would have to do would be to stand up, wrap an arm around the skid at the bottom of the helicopter, and let it carry me away. The canoe would go over the falls and shatter into a million pieces while Roland got it all on film. It was a simple gag that would seem very dramatic.

Still, I wanted to look it over for myself one more time. I threw on the dirty clothes I'd worn all day, pulled on my sneakers, and grabbed my room key. Quietly, I clicked the door behind me. Mom didn't wake up.

January in Niagara Falls is *cold*. It was a short walk to the observation deck. Some guy wearing a hat was out there, but he left by the time I got to the railing. I looked out over the falls. It wasn't illuminated, but the full moon lit it up pretty well.

When you see Niagara Falls on TV or in photos, it doesn't convey what an awesome sight it really is. The first time I'd been here, three years ago, I was too young to appreciate the beauty. I was overwhelmed by the power, the noise, the spray of the water when you get anywhere close to the edge.

When we were talking about the gag during the day, Roland told me how the falls came to be. Twenty million years ago, he explained, the Ice Age began and the polar ice caps crept across the planet. Glaciers swept down North America. Inch by inch, they gouged out the Great Lakes.

Through the centuries, the glaciers melted. About 12,000 years ago, huge torrents of water formed the Niagara River connecting Lake Erie and Lake Ontario. Little by little, the pounding water created this seven-mile canyon called the Niagara Gorge. It's still happening, actually. The falls has moved about seven miles upstream in 12,000 years. It was the nearby Indian tribes that named it "Niagara," which means "thundering water."

I was looking across the top of the Horseshoe Falls, where my canoe would be destroyed the next day. It's called the Horseshoe Falls because it's shaped like a big horseshoe. There are two falls here. The river forms a border between the United States and Canada, with Goat Island in the middle. The Horseshoe Falls is in Canada, and the American Falls is in the United States.

The Horseshoe is 176 feet high. That's eight feet lower than the

American Falls, but it's much more spectacular. Including the plunge basin beneath it, the total drop is 356 feet. It's a long way down. As I stood there on the observation deck, more than 200,000 cubic feet of water rushed by every second.

A freshwater gull flew by, and I imagined that she threw me a smirk. *She* wasn't worried about going over the falls. Following her flight path, I saw a figure at the other end of the observation deck. It appeared to be a man holding a cane in his right hand. I pretended not to notice the guy as I looked out at the falls, but I heard his footsteps scraping toward me. Suddenly I realized he was alongside me at the rail.

"John?"

Everybody who knows me calls me Johnny. There was only one person who ever called me John. I recognized the voice. I had gotten used to the idea that I would never hear it again. I turned to look at his face.

It was my dad.

Somehow, it didn't surprise me. We stared at each other for a moment.

"How's Squirt?" he asked.

"He's dead," I replied. "I thought you were dead too."

"So did I."

He wrapped his arms around me. He seemed so different from the man I remembered. So thin and frail. Dad used to have a crew cut, but now his hair was long and stringy. He was a little stooped over, and his hug didn't have the strength that I remembered. But then, I'm stronger than I was when I was ten.

"I *nearly* died," he said, his head on my shoulder. "The boat bounced off the rocks about halfway down and threw me into the basin. It broke nearly every bone in my body. But I managed to get to the Devil's Hole Ravine, a formation in the side of the gorge. I lay there for the longest time, thinking things over. It took about a year to get better."

So many feelings washed over me. Happiness. Astonishment. Exhilaration. You go through years thinking somebody you loved is gone forever, and then suddenly there they are, right next to you. It's a shock to the system.

"How did you know I would be here tonight?" I asked.

"Nobody can sleep the night before they go to the edge of the falls."

"But how did you know I was doing that?"

"I saw an article in the paper about them shooting the movie here."

All at once another feeling washed over me, replacing all those other feelings. *Anger*. I pushed Dad away from me, almost knocking him over.

"You've been alive all this time," I yelled, "and pretended you were dead!"

"John, I owed money to some people," he explained. "Bad people. I couldn't pay them back. They were going to hurt me. They might have hurt you too. I figured that if I was dead, my problem would be solved."

"So you just abandoned Mom?"

"The night before I went over the falls, your mother told me she wanted a divorce, John. We hadn't been getting along for some time. She never got used to me doing stunts, I guess, and finally she said she couldn't take it anymore. I figured that as long as we were splitting up, I might as well be out of the picture entirely. I changed my name and started a new life nearby here, in Canada."

"So *that's* why Mom doesn't like to talk about you," I said. "That's why she doesn't have any photos of you around the house. She never told me she was going to divorce you."

"I'm sure she didn't want to hurt you. It's bad enough for a kid to lose his father. He doesn't have to know his folks were going to split up."

"But I never saw you and Mom fight."

"You probably never saw us kiss either."

Everyone had always told me that my dad was the bravest man they ever met. He would jump off anything. He would run through fire. He would do any stunt, no matter how dangerous. He was fearless. But he was afraid to tell his own family that he was alive.

"You're a coward," I said.

"I suppose I am," Dad replied wearily.

"Do you expect Mom to take you back now? Is that why you came here?"

"No," he sighed, shaking his head. "She has a new life now."

"I could call the police, you know," I said. "I could go to the press. I could tell everybody."

"I know."

"Why did you come here?" I asked.

"To ask you not to do this gag."

"I'm doing it," I said, turning away from him.

"It's okay to hate me, John, but don't ignore me. This gag is too dangerous. There's a curse on these falls. They could kill you."

"They didn't kill *you*."

"They almost did. Look, I don't care if you do stunts for one year or twenty. Something will go wrong eventually. It's gonna catch up with you. If you do stunts for a living, you're gonna get hurt. Maybe you're gonna die. Did you ever hear of Dar Robinson?"

"No."

"Dar was a friend of mine. He was the greatest high-fall man ever. He jumped nine hundred feet off the CN Tower in Toronto. Once he jumped from the wing of a plane onto another plane flying beneath it. I saw him drive a car off the rim of the Grand Canyon and parachute down safely."

"He must have been a maniac," I said, marveling.

"He *wasn't* a maniac. That's the point. A maniac is an idiot who does something crazy and hopes he'll live to brag about it. A stuntman makes it *look* like he's doing something crazy. Dar Robinson never broke a bone in his body. Then one day he was doing a routine motorcycle gag and his bike slipped on some loose gravel. It went over a cliff. Dar was just thirty-nine."

"Accidents happen."

"Yeah, but especially if you do something foolish. John, it took a near fatal fall to get me to quit. You might not be so lucky. Let me tell you a story—"

"I've got to get some sleep," I said, waving him away. "I have a big day ahead of me."

"You're not going to sleep tonight," Dad insisted, walking unsteadily to a bench nearby. "Sit down. There's an old Indian legend you need to know about."

I followed him to the bench.

"Once," Dad explained, "people knew the wholeness of the world. They spoke with the earth and the sky. The sun, the moon, and the stars spoke with them. They knew the animals and the plants as their brothers and sisters. The Thunder beings taught them about what is and what will happen. People knew all these things, and knew the wholeness of the world."

"What's a Thunder being?" I asked.

"Don't interrupt," Dad continued. "Young Indian men who lived in Niagara used to demonstrate their courage by riding over the falls in birchbark canoes. Amazingly, they would be unharmed by the water."

"Why?"

"When they were behind the falls, they found themselves in a cave with a high ceiling and many creatures in it. These were the Thunder beings. They lived behind the falls and would lower the canoes gently to the base. There, the Thunder beings told the young men, 'You don't need to test yourselves this way. When you were created you were given all the courage and bravery that you will ever need.' The young men saw the wisdom in this, and they stopped testing themselves. But when white men arrived and pushed the Indians off the land, the Thunder beings moved away. People forgot their message. The earth and the stars and the animals continued to talk, but the white men didn't listen. As they forgot their oneness with the world, people became selfish, or mistrustful, or jealous of others. And that's where we are today, you and me. The Thunder beings, I believe, put a curse on these falls when they left. It makes white men want to go over them. In boats, in canoes, even in barrels. Most of them die."

"I'm doing the gag, Dad," I said.

Dad sighed. He knew he wasn't going to talk me out of it. Just as nobody could ever talk *him* out of all the crazy stunts he did when he was younger.

"Are you scared?" he asked.

"No," I stated firmly. "I know what I'm doing."

"If a stuntman isn't scared," Dad said, forcing me to make eye contact with him, "he's lost his respect for fear. *That's* dangerous. If you don't have a little fear, you don't belong out here tomorrow. When you become so sure of yourself, that's the time to quit."

"Why should I listen to *your* advice?" I demanded. "Like *your* judgment is so good? You walked out on me. You pretended you were dead."

"I'm sorry," he said. "It was the biggest mistake of my life. Just do me one favor. Don't do the gag, John."

"What favor did you ever do for *me*?"

I walked away. He struggled to catch up, and handed me a card with his phone number on it.

"If you need anything, you'll know how to reach me."

"I needed you three years ago," I said, and walked back to the hotel without looking back at him.

17

THE FIRST
SUBSTITUTE

I tossed and turned all night. At first, when I woke up in the morning, I thought it had all been a dream. Dad wasn't really alive. I hadn't met him on the observation deck.

But then, when Mom woke up and asked me how I managed to go to bed in pajamas and wake up in my clothes, I knew it was no dream.

"I went out for one last look at the falls," I explained. At least I was being honest, even if I didn't tell her the whole story.

"I don't suppose there's any point in begging you not to do the gag?" Mom asked hopefully.

"No, there isn't."

In fact, I was pumped. There's a feeling I always get when I'm about to do a big gag. It's a little bit nervousness, yes. But it's also a feeling of exhilaration. While millions of regular kids all over the world are playing video games and walking their dogs and taking piano lessons, I'm about to do something remarkable and amazing.

Something that no kid in the world has ever done. I like that feeling.

I would be putting myself in danger, but I had complete confidence in Roland. He had mapped it out. Every detail had been attended to. Except for my sprained ankle, I had never been hurt while working on one of Roland's movies. In fact, *nobody* had ever been seriously hurt while working on one of Roland's movies.

While Mom was in the shower, I went out to the parking lot to grab some breakfast from the food truck. Most of the *Two Birds, One Stone* cast and crew was already out there. I didn't see Augusta Wind or Ricky Corvette.

Everybody looked more serious than they usually do. A bit of tension hung in the air, it seemed to me. It's the tension that comes before something very dangerous is about to take place.

I had a feeling Dad might show up again and try to talk me out of doing the stunt. Sure enough, he hobbled over as I was munching a bagel.

"I just wanted to wish you good luck," he said.

"Thanks."

I didn't feel like being all buddy-buddy with him. A guy who abandons his family shouldn't be able to just stroll back in and expect his son to act like nothing happened.

"When did you get to be so big?" Dad asked, marveling at the reality that I was nearly as tall as he was.

"Must have been during the three years you were dead," I cracked.

I looked around to see if there was a way to get out of talking with Dad. That's when I noticed Mom about ten yards away, looking at us.

Oh no.

I would have thought Mom would faint or scream or something, seeing Dad alive after all that time. But she didn't. She just stood there, frozen, her mouth slightly open.

"Meredith!" Dad exclaimed, limping over to her. "You're as beautiful as ever." He went to kiss her, but she pulled her head back and folded her arms in front of her.

"And you're as . . . alive as ever, I see," Mom said coolly.

"You don't look very surprised to see me, Meredith."

"I'm not," Mom replied. "I always suspected you survived. Everybody always said you were indestructable, Joe."

"I'll take that as a compliment."

"What are you doing here?"

"I hoped to talk John out of doing this gag."

"It's useless," Mom said sadly. "He's as stubborn as you are."

I didn't know what to say. It was really weird and awkward seeing my mom and dad together again. Mom obviously didn't like it one bit. Dad looked like he was happy to see her, but clearly that wasn't the reason he had shown up.

"John," he said to me seriously, "I know I can't talk you out of doing this gag. But I want you to know something. I've been thinking about why it's so important to you to do it."

"Why?"

"Because I *couldn't* do it," he replied. "Remember that game we used to play when you were little? You would jump off the curb and I would jump off a chair, and then you would jump off the car and I would jump off something higher?"

"Yeah."

"Well, the game is over. You won, John. While I was gone these past three years, you accomplished more than I did in my entire career. You grew up to be a man. You don't have to prove that to me anymore."

His words rang in my ear like a bell. People always wondered why I did the crazy things I did. *I* always wondered why I did the crazy things I did. I never knew until that very instant. Suddenly it was all clear to me. I did what I did because I was trying to top my father.

At that moment, Roland strode over. "Ready to rock and roll, Johnny?" he asked excitedly.

"Roland Rivers, I want to introduce you to someone," I said. "This is Joe Thyme. My dad."

"Joe Thyme?! You're alive?" Roland said, trembling as he shook Dad's hand like he was meeting the Pope or something. "I—I've memorized all your films frame by frame. You have been my inspiration."

"Great," Dad said, unimpressed. "Look, Roland. The scene you're about to shoot is *not* going to work. This river moves thirty-seven, maybe thirty-nine miles an hour at the edge of the falls. There's no margin for error. If your helicopter is six inches too high, too far to the left or right, it will miss John. You obviously can't use a safety net in this scene. If John goes over the falls, there's a good chance his parachute will get tangled up in the rocks before it fully opens. It's too dangerous, and I know a thing or two about danger. I'm asking you as a professional—and as John's father—to call off the stunt."

Mom put her hand on Dad's shoulder in silent agreement.

Roland looked at my parents without saying anything. I could imagine what was going through his mind. My dad was probably the most daring stuntman in history. If *he* thinks a gag is too risky, it must be too risky. To send a thirteen-year-old boy into a situation like that—with the kid's parents standing there telling him not to— would be crazy.

On the other hand, *Two Birds, One Stone* was Roland's dream film. If he canceled the gag right now—after Paramount put so many millions of dollars into it—he would probably never get the chance to make a movie like this again. In fact, if Paramount was angry enough, Roland might not get the chance to make *any* movie again.

"You present me with a dilemma, Mr. Thyme."

Roland rubbed his beard and walked around in circles, as he always did when he had a tough choice to make. Finally, he whispered something into Dad's ear and picked up his bullhorn.

"Attention everyone!" Roland boomed over the parking lot. "Listen up."

Everybody in the cast and crew straggled over. Roland waited until the whole group had settled around him in a semicircle. He was about to speak when there was a commotion at the back of the crowd. I squinted my eyes to see what was going on.

Ricky Corvette was making his way up to the front.

"Ricky's gonna talk! Ricky's gonna talk! Ricky's gonna talk!" everybody buzzed.

Ricky whispered something to Roland, who nodded and handed him the bullhorn. Everybody leaned forward and hushed up quickly. Ricky hardly ever talks to *anybody*, unless they're very rich, very famous, or can help his career in some way.

"I have a short announcement to make," Ricky said. "I've given this a lot of thought, and I decided that I'm going to do the Niagara Falls gag *myself*."

Everybody laughed. Clearly, Ricky was trying to loosen us up a little. Break the tension. It was a classy move, I thought. Very un-Rickylike.

"No," he said a little more loudly. "I *mean* it. *I'm* going to do the gag."

He *meant* it! I couldn't believe what I was hearing. This might have been the biggest news to hit Niagara Falls since the Ice Age.

For a moment there was stunned silence. When everybody realized Ricky wasn't kidding and they got past the shock, the crowd started buzzing. It was as if it had just been announced that Christmas would be in July this year.

Roland was the first to get to Ricky. The Paramount lawyers were right behind, pulling out their cell phones and dialing frantically. The rest of the crew just sat there, shaking their heads in wonder.

My dad breathed a sigh of relief. Mom put her fists up over her head and looked up in the sky with her eyes closed, as if her prayers had been answered.

Ricky's mom let out a shriek, and then fainted. Somebody caught her before she hit the ground.

"My decision is final," Ricky said calmly. "So let's shoot the scene, shall we?"

"You're crazy!" Roland shouted at Ricky, gesturing wildly. "You have no experience doing this! You've had no training! It's suicide!"

"I know how to paddle a canoe," Ricky said. "I can do a chin-up on a bar. It doesn't look so tough."

"I refuse to be responsible for your safety," Roland said.

"*I'll* be responsible for my safety," Ricky replied.

"It's way too risky," one of the Paramount lawyers moaned. "This is a two-hundred-million dollar picture. We can't risk you getting hurt. The insurance company won't cover it. I won't allow it."

"Fine," Ricky said, getting up to leave. "Then get yourself another movie star. Either I do the stunt myself, or you can take my name off the credits."

"Wait!" the other Paramount lawyer cried. "You mean you want to sit in the canoe, right? Then they pluck you out of the water and Johnny will do the helicopter part, right?"

"Wrong," Ricky insisted. "I'm doing the whole gag from start to finish."

Ricky had a determined look on his face. There seemed to be no talking him out of doing the gag himself. Nobody could do anything about it. Paramount had invested too much money in the film to shut the whole production down. Ricky, the star that he was, had the power to do whatever he wanted to do.

But nobody ever thought he would do *this*. Up until now, Ricky had always been content to have me replace him in any scene that didn't call for a close-up.

The Paramount lawyers did some frenetic cell-phoning to their bosses. They made Ricky sign a piece of paper saying Paramount wouldn't be responsible if he got hurt. When they were done jawing, they went over and talked to Roland. He shook his head a few times, and then picked up his bullhorn.

"Okay, people!" Roland announced, waiting for everyone to quiet down. "Money talks, I guess. Instead of Mr. Hangtime being the stunt double for Mr. Corvette, Mr. Corvette will do his own stunt. Let's set up for the shot."

Everybody started moving their gear toward their places around the Horseshoe Falls. The camera guys set up on the observation deck, on Goat Island, at the base of the falls, and on the Rainbow Bridge. There would also be a camera in the helicopter that would be scooping Ricky up just before the canoe went over the falls.

The emergency crew took up stations all over. There were two ambulances, doctors, nurses, a full medical staff. Boats got in position downstream from the falls in case they had to pull Ricky out.

Everyone looked grim, nervous, serious.

I wasn't sure what to do with myself. Usually, I spend the minutes before a gag thinking it over in my head. Running it through one last time to make sure I don't mess up.

As I watched everyone getting ready, it occurred to me that I felt a certain amount of relief in knowing I would not be going to the brink of the falls. It was the first time in memory that I wasn't itching to get out there and do a gag. I didn't have to top my dad anymore.

At the same time, an unpleasant thought came to me. If something happened to Ricky Corvette doing the gag, it would be partly *my* fault. If I hadn't told Ricky off when he told me to get him a Mountain Dew, he probably wouldn't have decided to do this.

I ran over and caught up with Ricky as he was walking toward the helicopter that would take him upstream to begin the gag.

"Ricky!" I shouted. "Look, I'm sorry about what I said yesterday. I was just mouthing off. It was stupid."

"Forget it," Ricky said, without breaking stride. "This isn't about you. I've been thinking about it for a long time."

"Let me do the gag for you this time," I suggested. "Then maybe on the next movie you could do some car gags. Jumps. Falls. You know, get used to doing your own stunts."

"If I don't do this *now*," he insisted, "there may *be* no next movie."

"You don't have to do this, Ricky. You don't have to prove how tough you are."

"Yes, I *do*."

Ricky stopped and looked at me. It may have been the first time he ever spoke to me man to man.

"I'm so envious of you," he said. "Everybody knows you've done all the hard stuff for me. People think I'm a fraud, and they're right. I could always smile for the camera and look cute. But I can't get away with that now. I'm not a kid anymore. If I don't do this, my career is over."

"If you *do* it, your *life* may be over," I said.

"My career *is* my life."

Despite everything that happened between me and Ricky, I actually felt sorry for him. We walked in silence the rest of the way to the helicopter. When we got there, Dad was helping the pilot and cameraman load equipment into the chopper.

"Get in!" Dad yelled over the roar of the rotors.

Ricky put on his helmet and strapped on the life vest. It was a specially designed vest that had a parachute in the back. The chute didn't even have a cord to pull. There's a computer chip in it that can sense downward acceleration. If the person wearing it suddenly drops ten feet, the chute opens automatically.

The chopper took all of us two miles upstream, where the canoe was waiting. A guy was tinkering with a tiny video camera that had been mounted on the front of the canoe. The camera would be destroyed, of course, when the canoe tumbled over the falls. But it would shoot some incredible video first, and beam it over to a truck in the parking lot.

"Don't stand up in the canoe," Dad instructed Ricky as he stepped off the helicopter. "It will rock too much. Wait for the helicopter to come low enough for you to grab on, okay?"

"Okay," Ricky replied.

"Good luck."

"Thanks, man," Ricky said, shaking Dad's hand.

Roland was in position on the observation deck overlooking the Horseshoe Falls, so he could be as close as possible to the edge. He had walkie-talkie communications with all the cameramen.

"Sure you want to do this, Ricky?" Roland asked through the helicopter's walkie-talkie.

"I'm sure."

"Then we're ready when you are. Roll cameras!"

Ricky put a foot in the canoe and pushed off. I gave the canoe a shove for good measure. There was no turning back now. I scampered back aboard the helicopter and we lifted off. The helicopter would shadow Ricky and rescue him at the edge of the falls.

The current was moving swiftly, much more swiftly than an ordinary river. Once Ricky paddled out to the middle, he didn't need to paddle at all. The current just pulled him along. The chopper pilot kept pace with Ricky, about ten feet in front of him and thirty feet above the water. He told me we were moving at thirty-six miles per hour. So far, so good.

From where I was above the river, I could see the Horseshoe Falls a mile and a half ahead. I knew Ricky couldn't see it, and that was probably for the better. It was frightening enough being in the river without having to see the point where the river suddenly drops away.

The water started getting choppier about a mile from the Horseshoe. I could see the canoe bobbing up and down. I didn't know how much canoeing experience Ricky had. You could probably never have enough experience to prepare yourself for *this*.

"Be ready to pick him up early in case he capsizes or chickens out," Dad yelled to the pilot.

"Camera number one," Roland barked, "are you on him?"

"Affirmative," the pilot replied.

"Camera number two. Can you see him yet?"

"Affirmative."

"Camera number three—"

"Not yet, Roland." A voice crackled over the radio. "Wait, I see him now!"

The helicopter was one hundred yards from the falls. The pilot accelerated, rushing ahead of Ricky's canoe to get into position for the rescue. Between the sound of the 'copter and the sound of the falls, it was so loud my ears were ringing.

We were hovering at the edge of the Horseshoe, and the view was incredible. When I looked out one side of the chopper, I could see Ricky's canoe coming toward us. Out the other side, there was nothing. Just a long way down.

"This is awesome!" the cameraman hollered.

"Stop sightseeing!" Dad barked. "Bring it *down*!"

The pilot lowered the chopper until I could feel the spray of water in my face.

"Lower!" Dad shouted. "Lower!"

"I'm only five feet over the top!" the pilot shouted back. "Any lower and we'll hit it."

"Get ready to make the scoop!" Roland hollered over the walkie-talkie.

I could see Ricky's face now, the fear in his eyes. The canoe was bouncing and bumping through the whitewater like a Ping-Pong ball. It was heading a little to the left of us. The pilot moved over so the canoe would slide right below us.

"Grab it!" Dad screamed to Ricky when he was close enough to hear. "Grab hold!"

Ricky reached up for the skid on the bottom of the helicopter. He missed it at first, then stood up so he could reach. He wrapped his fingers around the skid, the way you do when you do a chin-up.

"Wrap your *arm* around it!" Dad yelled down to him. A chin-up hold, I knew, wouldn't be strong enough.

"If you've got him, go!" Roland yelled. "Go!"

Ricky was hanging on to the skid with both hands, trying to pull himself up so he could wrap an arm around it. I could see in his face that he was struggling. He didn't have the arm strength. He probably never played on monkey bars in his life. The pilot lifted up the helicopter and moved away from the edge of the Horseshoe.

That's when Ricky's fingertips slipped off the skid.

18

THE SECOND SUBSTITUTE

I saw the look of terror on Ricky's face as his fingertips slipped off the skid. I saw his mouth open to scream, but the noise of the water and rotors drowned it out. And then I watched Ricky fall.

I may not have liked Ricky Corvette, but you don't want to wish something like *this* on your worst enemy. There was nothing I could do to help him. Dad spat out a four-letter word that you've probably heard but won't see here.

"We missed him!" the cameraman screamed.

"Good Lord in heaven!" Roland yelled over the walkie-talkie.

The parachute popped out of Ricky's life jacket. Because the helicopter had moved away from the falls before Ricky fell, the chute had just enough room to open. I watched it drop.

"Get him out of there as soon as he hits the water!" Roland ordered. "Get an ambulance ready!"

Sirens were screaming when our helicopter landed in the parking lot. Everyone there was running in all directions. Police cars had arrived.

By the time Ricky hit the bottom, I was told, four rescue boats were already chugging toward the churning water. They got as close to the falls as they could without capsizing. For a few anxious seconds, there was no sign of Ricky's body.

Finally, one of the rescue divers spotted Ricky, bobbing up and down lifelessly in the whitewater. Ten divers dove in and pulled him out.

In seconds, they had Ricky in the boat and the boat sped back to the dock. An ambulance was waiting there. A paramedic crew carried Ricky into the ambulance and slammed the back doors shut. It screeched off. Three cop cars, sirens blasting and lights flashing, provided an escort to the hospital.

There was no way of knowing if Ricky was dead or alive. It depended on how he hit the rocks at the bottom of the falls.

All we could do was wait. Filming was suspended for the day, of course. The crew was walking around in a daze. The helicopter pilot looked worse than anyone. Everyone told him it wasn't his fault, but I'm sure he was wondering what would happen to him if Ricky died.

When I found Roland, he was just sitting on a chair under a tree. He looked like he was in shock.

"Nobody has *ever* been seriously hurt on a Roland Rivers film," he said, staring off into space. "*Ever*."

In a few minutes, somebody from the hospital called the set. Everybody gathered around the phone.

Ricky was alive, we were informed. He was busted up pretty badly, though. Both arms and legs were broken. There were some internal injuries. His face was messed up, and he would be under-going surgery to reconstruct it. The doctors were going to have to build him a new nose, taking cartilage from his ears and skin from his neck. Ricky was conscious, but just barely.

"He was lucky," somebody said.

Lucky? If falling over Niagara Falls from a helicopter is good luck, I wondered what bad luck might be. If anybody was lucky, it was *me*.

A few minutes after the phone call from the hospital came in, my father came over to the bench where I was sitting.

"You okay?" he asked, sitting down next to me.

"Yeah."

"This Corvette fellow," Dad asked, "is he a friend of yours?"

"He's just a movie star," I replied. "He barely knows my name."

"That's the way it is with movie stars. I'm just glad it wasn't you."

We sat there for a few minutes without talking. The crew had begun packing up their lights and other gear and loading it onto trucks. It was uncomfortable. I didn't know if I would ever see my dad again, or if I *wanted* to. It was still kind of shocking to realize he was alive.

I finally broke the ice. "I guess maybe I should have listened to you."

"About what?"

"Doing the gag," I said. "It was too dangerous. I could have been killed."

"We all make mistakes," Dad replied. "You just have to get on with your life."

I looked at Dad. He had made a mistake too, in abandoning me. I realized that he was trying to get on with *his* life, and contacting me again was part of that. I stuck out my hand and he shook it.

"I'm sorry about what I did, son."

As Mom and I silently packed up our clothes to go back to California that night, I knew what she was thinking. It could have been *me*. *I* could have been the one in the canoe. *I* could have missed the grab. *I* could have been the one barely conscious in the hospital.

I could have been less lucky than Ricky. I could have been killed.

There was a knock on the hotel-room door and Mom opened it. It was Roland, with the Paramount lawyers. They came in and made some small talk, making sure to express their concern for Ricky. Then the Paramount guys got to the point.

"As you know, the studio has spent a small fortune on *Two Birds, One Stone*," one of them said. "We were counting on it to be our biggest blockbuster this year."

"The movie was almost finished when Ricky had his unfortunate accident," the other lawyer said. "We can't afford to abandon it."

"So you want to reshoot the canoe gag with me in Ricky's place?" I asked.

"No!" Mom announced. "I won't let Johnny do that scene!"

"That won't be necessary, Mrs. Thyme," the first lawyer said. "Roland believes he can rewrite the ending and use the footage he already shot."

"So why are you guys here?" I asked.

"Johnny," Roland said, "remember those seven lines of dialogue Ricky was supposed to say? We still have to shoot them. They want *you* to take Ricky's place in the acting scenes."

Acting scenes? I couldn't *act*! I hadn't acted since I was in my third-grade play. Even then, I only had to play a tree. Roland had to be joking.

"Johnny," one of the lawyers said, "Ricky Corvette's career is over. I saw his face at the hospital, and believe me, he will never play a leading man again. Frankly, his career may have been over even *before* the accident. He was getting older and his voice had changed. As much as we all hate to admit it, Ricky's looks and that cute voice were all he had."

I looked at Mom. She shrugged.

"You've already appeared in all the other scenes of the movie," the other lawyer said, more excitedly. "*You're* the real star, Johnny. We want *Two Birds, One Stone* to be a Johnny Hangtime movie. Naturally, you will be compensated appropriately—say, one million dollars—and receive star billing."

A *million dollars?* My allowance was ten dollars a week. I couldn't even imagine what a million dollars *looked* like.

"You only have to say seven lines of dialogue, Johnny," Roland assured me.

Seven lines of dialogue. I would have to *speak* seven lines. In front of a camera. Shooting close-ups of my face. And a crew. And millions of people would see it.

I wondered if somebody had turned up the heat in the room. Beads of sweat gathered on my forehead. I could feel it under my arms too.

This was silly, I thought to myself. In the last four years I had been run over by trucks, hit by machine-gun fire, thrown through plate glass windows, and drowned in quicksand. But none of those things frightened me as much as the thought of saying seven lines of dialogue.

Seven lines. A million dollars. I began to feel lightheaded, woozy. And that was the last thing I remembered.

19

A PRESENT

When I came to, I looked around and saw I was in a hospital room. Oh, come on, Mom! I thought. You didn't have to put me in the hospital just because I *fainted*!

I looked to my right and saw I had a roommate. The poor guy was bandaged up from head to toe, like a mummy. He couldn't even turn his head.

"Hi," I said softly, not sure if the guy was awake.

"Hi," he replied.

"What happened to *you*?"

"I fell."

"Must have been a pretty bad fall," I said.

"Yeah, over Niagara Falls."

"Ricky!" I exclaimed. "It's me, Johnny Hangtime!"

"What happened to *you*?"

"I must have passed out," I explained. "The last thing I remember, Roland was asking me to take your place for the acting scenes."

Ricky laughed, even though I could tell it was painful for him. "Roland told me he was going to ask you," he said, still giggling. "That cracks me up. You're not afraid to jump off the Empire State Building. You're not afraid to go over Niagara Falls. But you're afraid to say a few lines."

"It's scary."

"What *you* do is scary," Ricky said. "Until yesterday, I never appreciated how tough it is to do what you do. Any jerk can read lines. Doing stunts is another thing."

"A lot of guys wouldn't have had the guts to try that gag," I told him. "You've got guts."

Ricky's mouth curved up in a little smile. "Hey, stunt kid," he said. "I got you a little present. Open the drawer next to you."

I opened the drawer of the night table between the two beds. There was a box in there, about the size of a shoe box. It was wrapped, and had a bow around it. I peeled off the paper and opened the box.

Inside was a can of Mountain Dew. The note with it read: "To Johnny Hangtime: Thanks for making me a movie star. Now it's your turn."

I cracked open the can and chugged half of it. Then I held it up to Ricky's mouth so he could have some too.

"Break a leg," Ricky said. "But not like I did."

ACTING

Roland gathered the cast and crew at the Rainbow Bridge, where we were to shoot the last two scenes of *Two Birds, One Stone*. The wardrobe people dressed me in clothes that looked just like the clothes Ricky was wearing when he went over the falls. I was drenched with water, so I'd look like I just climbed out of the river.

"Okay," Roland explained, "I rewrote the script a little, so let me set the scene for you, Johnny. You survived the falls, but Augusta is dead. Well, she's not *really* dead, but you *think* she's dead. You crawl out of the water and flop down on the bank. Go ahead."

I looked at my script. . . .

BOBBY
(sobbing)
Why, why, why did you have to die?
You meant so much to me!
I loved you. I'll never forget you.

"Are you kidding, Roland?" I asked. "I have to say this?"

"Yes, and with feeling. Quiet everybody. Roll camera!"

"Why, why, why did you have to die?" I moaned. "You meant so much to me! I loved you. I'll never forget you."

"Cut!" Roland shouted. "Johnny, you look like you're acting."

"I *am* acting."

"I need for you to act without looking like you're acting. I need real emotion here. Try thinking of something sad. I'm sure you have some bad memories you can dredge up from the recesses of your brain. Let's try it again. Roll camera!"

I thought of all the sad things that had happened to me. Like the time some kid beat me up in third grade when I wouldn't let him cheat off me in a spelling test. And the time I left my baseball card collection on a bus and never saw it again. I thought of how I felt when Dad went over Niagara Falls and we all thought he was dead. I thought of how I felt when Dad showed up again and told me that he and Mom never really got along. And then I thought of Squirt.

So much had happened, I had almost forgotten about Squirt's death. When we finished the movie and went back home, it would be the first time Squirt wouldn't be there. Tears started welling up in my eyes.

All my life I had trained myself not to cry. Dad always said crying was for babies. Big boys didn't do it. But I felt tears coming on and for the first time I didn't try to stop them. I was going to wipe them away, but I didn't. That made them worse. My eyes were all watery and I couldn't see out of them, and I started to weep. I couldn't control myself.

"Why, why, *why* did you have to die?" I moaned. "You meant so much to me! I loved you. I'll never forget you. I used to love the way your hooves clattered down the gravel road. The way—"

"Cut!" Roland yelled. "Beautiful, Johnny! We'll just cut that part out about the hooves. It will be great. You're a natural!"

Everybody gave me a standing ovation. Roland gave me a big hug and handed me the new last page of the script. . . .

Jennifer embraces Bobby.

BOBBY
(shocked)
You're alive! I can't believe it!

JENNIFER
(stroking his hair)
I couldn't die without you.
Just as I can't live without you.

BOBBY
And now you've given
me a reason to live.

Bobby and Jennifer kiss.

I had to read that last part twice. *Bobby and Jennifer kiss.* Nobody mentioned to me that there was a *kissing* scene. Not that I was opposed to it or anything, but . . .

"Roland," I said, tapping him on the shoulder. "I need to talk to you about something. In private."

"What is it?" he asked as he walked me toward the road.

"This is kind of embarrassing, but I . . . I've never kissed a girl before."

"Hmm," Roland said, rubbing his beard. "This could pose some problems. I could cut the scene . . . "

"No!" I protested. "It's just that she's . . . "

"So beautiful?" Roland asked. "Perhaps I could get some really ugly girls for you to practice with. Then you could work your way up to Augusta?"

"No," I said. "She's Ricky Corvette's *girlfriend*. And he's lying in a hospital bed—"

"Ricky's girlfriend?" Roland roared with laughter. "Ricky and Augusta *despise* each other! That boyfriend/girlfriend nonsense is merely gossip twaddle to keep them in the news. Just pucker up and do what comes naturally. You'll be fine."

A limousine pulled up and Augusta Wind got out, looking like an angel. Her mother quickly followed, wearing earrings that were so big, I wondered why they didn't rip her earlobes off.

"Roland!" Augusta's mother shouted, waving her script. "I need to have a word with you!"

"Yes, Marcia?" Roland walked over to her, like a man on the way to his own execution.

"What's the meaning of this?" she asked. "I didn't send my daughter to acting school for four years so she could kiss a *stunt boy*!"

She said *stunt boy* almost like she were saying *vermin*.

"Who was it," Roland asked, "that you sent your daughter to acting school to kiss?"

"A star, like Ricky Corvette, you twit!"

"Marcia, as you very well know, Ricky Corvette is unavailable. Johnny is taking his place, and I'm sure he will do an excellent—"

"Augusta's not happy, Roland!" her mother said angrily. "Nowhere in her contract does it say she has to kiss any stunt boys."

Suddenly, Augusta broke out of the comatose cloud she always seemed to walk around in. She glared at her mother.

"That's it!" she shouted, waving her arms around. "I've had it! I'll kiss anyone I want!"

With that, Augusta wrapped her arms around me, bent me backward, and kissed me hard on the lips. I was too surprised to do anything but gasp.

"How do you like that, Mother?" Augusta yelled. "I'm almost sixteen years old! You can't control my life anymore. I'm not some mannequin that you can cart around and pose any way you want!"

"Augusta Wind!" her mother said, shocked. "How *dare* you speak to me in that tone of voice!"

"My name is *not* Augusta Wind," Augusta said. "That stupid name was *your* idea. My name is Gladys Shmutz, and that's what I want to be called from this moment on."

Gladys Shmutz?

"How could you?" Mrs. Wind—I mean, Mrs. Shmutz—moaned. "I've been grooming you to be a star since you were three! When I think of all the money I spent on ballet school, hair stylists, singing lessons, makeup, photographers, nutritionists, tutors. And this is how you treat me?"

"Leave me alone!" Gladys yelled. "I want you *out* of my life! I never asked for any of those things! All I ever wanted to do was go out and play like a normal girl!"

And then she stormed off down the road.

Man, what an exit! Those four years of acting school really paid off. I felt like *she* should get a standing ovation. I would give her an Oscar for Best Actress in a minute.

Roland led the disraught Mrs. Shmutz back to the limo and sent it back to the hotel. Then he retrieved Gladys and set up the scene. I had to lie down against a rock, looking half dead. Gladys knelt down and held me. All the camera guys, gaffers, grips, and everybody else were standing around staring at us. There must have been fifty people watching.

"Hello," I said to Gladys as Roland monkeyed with the camera. "I'm Johnny Thyme. I don't think we've ever been formally introduced."

"I'm Gladys," she smiled. "It's nice to meet you. I was always too shy to come over and—"

"Okay, enough chitchat," Roland called. "Roll camera!"

"You're alive!" I emoted. "I can't believe it!"

"I couldn't die without you," Gladys replied. "Just as I can't live without you."

"And now you've given me a reason to live."

Gladys put both arms around my neck and slowly moved her face to mine until our lips met. As we held it, my heart was beating so fast, I thought my chest was going to explode.

"Cut!" Roland yelled.

I didn't look at Gladys. It was too embarrassing. I was ready to get up, but Roland held up his hand.

"Okay, let's try that again, everyone," he announced. "Move the light a little to the right to pick up Augusta's face."

"Again?" I asked.

"Johnny, it's not like falling off the Statue of Liberty, where you have to get it right in one take. We might have to shoot this scene over and over all afternoon until we get it perfect."

"Do I get paid each time?" I joked. "That's the way it always worked before."

Gladys punched me on the arm, but she was smiling.

"If he doesn't want to kiss her, I'd be happy to take over," one of the cameramen shouted. Everybody laughed.

Roland was right. I did just fine. In fact, after about ten takes, Gladys and I had gotten so good at kissing that we were still doing it after Roland yelled "Cut!" Finally he had to tap us on our shoulders and tell us to knock it off.

21

THE THIRD SUBSTITUTE

Two Birds, One Stone came out a few months later. I went to the premiere in Hollywood with Mom and Gladys. It was really cool, even though I had to wear a tuxedo and my neck itched the whole time. My name was up on the marquee in big letters. Flashes were popping all over the place when Gladys and I got out of the limo.

Going to school Monday morning after the movie opened was really strange. Instead of Boris Bonner waiting on the front steps to beat me up, there was an enormous banner:

CONGRATULATIONS JOHNNY HANGTIME!

Everybody swarmed all over me, shaking my hand and pounding me on the back. Some of the teachers even came over and asked for my autograph. Suddenly I had more friends than I knew what to do with. And all the girls who used to totally ignore me were gawking at me with this goofy look in their eyes that I had never seen before.

I guess being in movies suddenly makes a guy a lot better-looking.

At the end of the day, after I had signed about three hundred autographs, I went to my locker to get my books. Everyone else had gone home by then. The peace and quiet felt good.

And then Boris Bonner came over.

I knew I would have to deal with him at some point. I wondered what he would say to me now that he knew the truth about why I couldn't take gym class, why I never went to dances, why I used to be such a bore at school.

Bonner reached into his pocket and pulled out a few dollar bills.

"I'm sorry about the way I treated you," he said, holding the money out to me. "I didn't realize you were cool. If you'll forgive me, I'd like to be friends."

I looked at him. I could take the money. I could also spit in his face. It was my choice.

"Don't ever treat anybody that way again," I warned Bonner. "Whether you think they're cool or not."

And then I walked away.

Two Birds, One Stone made something like sixty million dollars the first weekend, and broke box-office records all over the country. Right away, Paramount started planning the sequel, *Three Birds, Two Stones*.

So, picture this: I'm standing on the 103rd-floor "Skydeck" of the Sears Tower in downtown Chicago. This building—the second tallest in the world—has 16,100 windows, 25,000 miles of plumbing, 2,000 miles of electrical wire, and 43,000 miles of telephone cable.

They don't call it the Windy City for nothing. I can barely hold on up here. Below, Lake Michigan looks like an ocean. In the distance, I can see parts of Indiana, Michigan, and Wisconsin. The Skydeck is 1,353 feet above the ground.

And I'm about to jump off it.

Here's the plot of *Three Birds, Two Stones*: A gang of drug dealers has taken over the Sears Tower. They're armed, and they've taken positions on every tenth floor. Augusta Wind—or, I should say, Gladys Shmutz—is tied up in the lobby, and they're planning to torture her.

I have to jump from the Skydeck with a hang glider on my back. As I corkscrew around and around the building on my way down, I'll have to pick off the drug dealers one at a time with my machine gun. After I land, I'll blow away the leader in the lobby and rescue Gladys.

Truly, this is the coolest gag I have *ever* been asked to do.

Yet, somehow, something doesn't feel right. Ever since I met Dad at Niagara Falls, I realize, my heart hasn't been into stunting.

It's too late to back out now. Helicopters are in the air, hovering around the building on all sides. The crew has their cameras in position. Roland's got his bullhorn in his hand. Mom's got her fingers crossed. I give my harness one last yank to make sure it's tight all around.

"Ready, Johnny?" Roland asks.

"I guess."

"Nervous?"

"A little."

"It's a piece of cake," Roland assures me. "I'll meet you at Dairy Queen. Roll cameras!"

I take a deep breath. I'm about to lean forward off the ledge.

Suddenly, a guy with a briefcase comes running over.

"Wait!" he screams, all out of breath. "Don't jump!"

"Stop cameras!" Roland yells. "Hold everything!"

I exhale and come back off the ledge. The guy with the briefcase rushes over to me. I recognize him as one of the Paramount lawyers. There is a teenage kid behind him.

"We've decided . . . " the Paramount guy huffs, gasping for breath, " . . . it's way too dangerous . . . for Johnny . . . to be doing this gag. Especially . . . after what happened to Ricky Corvette. So we hired a stuntkid . . . to take Johnny's place."

"You hired somebody to do stunts in place of *me*?" I ask, a wave of relief sweeping over my body.

"Johnny, you're a star now," the lawyer explains. "The studio can't risk something happening to you. I believe your days as a stunt-kid are over."

Well, Mom lets out this shriek of joy that could probably shatter every one of those 16,100 windows in the Sears Tower. She hugs Roland and grabs me, almost knocking the breath out of me.

"Mom! No kissing, okay?" I protest.

"Meredith," Roland says to Mom, "perhaps this would be an opportune moment to invite you to have dinner with me this evening. I know of a marvelous steak house on Rush Street—"

"You've got a date, Roland," Mom replies quickly.

The teenage kid who was with the lawyer steps forward and sticks out his hand. "Mr. Hangtime," he says to me, "my name is Bobby Holiday. I've seen all your movies. Dude, you're my idol. I'm an adrenaline junkie, and I'm totally stoked about taking your place."

I help Bobby put on the hang glider and show him how to work the fake machine gun. Roland explains the gag to him carefully and Bobby steps out onto the ledge.

"Roll cameras!" Roland shouts.

"We'll meet you at Pizza Hut," I call to Bobby. He looks puzzled, and I add, "I'll explain later." I give Bobby the thumbs-up sign. He leans forward, pushes off with his legs, and he's gone.

I lean over the edge of the Skydeck and watch Bobby glide around and around the building like a paper airplane, spitting out sparks of machine-gun fire as he goes. As he disappears from view, I realize that I'm not wishing it was me. And it feels good.

AFTERWARD . . .

Well, you can probably guess what happened with everybody afterward.

Mom: Fell in love with Roland.

Roland: Fell in love with Mom. He also decided to quit making action movies. He said being in love with Mom gave him all the endorphins he needed.

So Roland started making art films. He's currently working on *My Dinner With Andre, Part II*. It's about two guys who sit around a table talking for two hours. Mom says Roland is a genius.

Ricky Corvette: He's getting better slowly, and it looks like he's going to make a full recovery. Ricky's movie-star days are over, but when I talked to him about that, I got the feeling that he was almost glad. He's anxious to start his life over as a normal person.

Gladys Shmutz: She gave up movies entirely. She's not sure what she's going to do with her life yet. In the meantime, she has enrolled in public high school and says she wants to go to college. All the newspapers say we're going steady.

Mrs. Shmutz and Ricky's mom: Who cares? Ricky and Gladys moved out of their houses and stopped speaking to their parents.

Boris Bonner: I wouldn't know. Every time he sees me, he crosses the street or ducks into a classroom.

Me: I've been living the tough life of a movie star. You know, hanging out with Gladys. Shooting a movie or making a personal appearance every once in a while. Counting the money I rake in from the Johnny Hangtime action figures, trading cards, lunch boxes, and backpacks. Buying lots of stuff I don't need.

Dad: I'm not sure. I still have the card he gave me on the observation deck at Niagara Falls. I've been thinking about him just about every day lately. I think I might give him a call.